"YOU LOOKING FOR A WAY TO KILL THE NIGHT?"

The girl smiled at Johnny as she asked the question. Then she sucked in a deep breath, and her sweater expanded in the darkness, high and full, straining.

"You got any ideas?" he said. He wasn't sure of her. Had she heard about him? Did she know he was the one the cops were after?

"I got a room on Lex," she said. "Not the Waldorf, but clean sheets. And a price that's right."

"Like?"

"Like five for a roll, and seven-fifty for all night. You got seven-fifty?"

"I've got seven-fifty."

"Don't let the price throw you, man," she said, grinning in the darkness. "It's quality merchandise. I'm feeling generous. . . ."

Other SIGNET Mysteries
by Ed McBain

RUNAWAY BLACK

by
Ed McBain

*(originally published under
the pseudonym Richard Marsten)*

A SIGNET BOOK
NEW AMERICAN LIBRARY
TIMES MIRROR

SIGNET TRADEMARK REG. U.S. PAT. OFF. AND FOREIGN COUNTRIES
REGISTERED TRADEMARK—MARCA REGISTRADA
HECHO EN CHICAGO, U.S.A.

SIGNET, SIGNET CLASSICS, MENTOR, PLUME
AND MERIDIAN BOOKS
*are published by The New American Library, Inc.,
1301 Avenue of the Americas, New York, New York 10019*

FIRST SIGNET PRINTING, FEBRUARY, 1978

1 2 3 4 5 6 7 8 9

PRINTED IN THE UNITED STATES OF AMERICA

To Bobby and Jerry

Chapter One

Because the neighborhood had planted fear so deeply inside him, he ran the instant he heard the shot.

He did not stop to wonder where the shot had come from. A shot meant trouble, and trouble meant cops, and in the neighborhood you ran when the cops came.

He came up out of The Valley, away from the slab-gray fronts of the tenements, away from the back yards and the clothes stiff with the first rush of winter, grotesquely clutching the cold air. His feet clattered on the pavement, and a hundred hollow echoes reverberated from the cast-iron sky, fled into dim hallways, reached out again to smother the asphalt with sound. He went past the candy store on the corner where Freddie ran a drop, and then he hit Seventh Avenue and turned downtown, slowing his pace a little now because the shot was behind him. He mingled with the crowd, and there was warmth in the crowd, and he heard the click of high heels on pavement, smelled the perfume of the women, listened to the voices disjointed and distorted, a part of his people now, a part of the warm cocoon bundled around him, bundled against the winter and the cops and the shot he had heard.

The Market Place was ahead of him, stretching down to the park from 115th Street. He had been to the Market only once, when he was sixteen, and he could still remember the dim hallway and the lightly perfumed body, the shadows on the ceiling, the heavily murmured incantation of commercial love. He had enjoyed the experience, but there was plenty around you didn't have to pay for, and he knew plenty of guys who'd been lured into a hallway by a pair of loose hips on

1

the Market, only to be slashed and mugged by accomplices. And though he knew all this, the Market still held a peculiar fascination for him, and he almost forgot the shot as he walked through it.

The girl lounging in one of the doorways, lighting a cigarette, showing colossal disinterest for everything around her, shoved herself off the doorjamb with an insinuating push of her hip. She started down the steps in front of the building, swinging her body exaggeratedly, and he watched the smooth flow of silk over her flat stomach where the monkey-fur jacket ended. He quickened his pace, and she touched his arm lightly as he passed her. She didn't say anything. She tilted her face and smiled an age-old smile, and he simply shook his head and kept walking, and then she cursed after him.

He walked through the Market, wondering what was going on in each of the rooms behind the drawn window shades, knowing very well what was going on, but wondering about it anyway, and deriving a strange peculiar satisfaction from wondering.

The Golden Edge faced Central Park, and he thought, Next to Sugar Hill, I'll take the Golden Edge. The thought was not a new one to him, and he shrugged the way he always did whenever it crossed his mind. He knew he lived in The Valley, and he knew that he'd probably die in The Valley, unless he made a big killing on the numbers, and then, man, watch that Caddy. A big yellow job, with whitewall tires, and maybe zebra upholstery. No, maybe that would be putting it on too much. But yellow, anyway, and whitewalls for sure. And then watch all the pussies wail when Johnny Lane came down the street. A convertible with the top down, and he'd smile at them and just wave, sort of, not a real wave, just a kind of raising of his hand a little to let them know he was born and raised here and he bled for them all, but he was glad he was out of it. And then he'd cut out for his pad on Sugar Hill, none of this Golden Edge stuff, not if he made a real killing, and he'd have a Scandi-

2

navian maid, or maybe a German *Frau* who just came to this country and couldn't speak English so good, one of those real blonde women, sort of big all over, with one of those can't-speak-English smiles on her face, willing to please, happy to please, she damn well better please or he'd get him another one. And Cindy —well, Cindy'd live there with him, of course, but she wouldn't mind the *Frau* because she'd understand, Cindy would. That's if he made a killing, or if he could latch onto something the way Barney did, but he always had a horseshoe up his behind, that guy.

He crossed 110th Street and walked into the park, not looking behind him because looking behind was the worst thing you could do. He found an empty bench, and he sat down and pulled his coat collar up against the cold, and only then did he wonder who got shot. Maybe nobody at all, and maybe there was no reason to run, but when cops are involved, it's better to run first and think about it afterward, or just run and not think about it at all. He wondered if the cops ever worked you over for just thinking about something, and he smiled at his own absurd imagination and tried to make himself comfortable on the bench.

He had never liked the winter, and he sure as hell wasn't looking forward to this one. Last winter they hadn't had enough heat to keep a cockroach alive, though the cockroaches didn't seem to care about the heat. Molly kept the oven lit all the time last winter, and you could suffocate from that kind of dry, catch-in-the-throat gas heat. You'd think that sonovabitch would at least give you heat, especially in the winter, instead of making your muscles sore from pounding on the goddamned radiator all the time. He was almost ashamed to bring Cindy up there, and he remembered the time she didn't want to take off her clothes, and he thought it was because Molly would be home soon, but it was really because the flat was so cold.

He pulled his collar higher. If anything, this was going to be a colder winter. He could feel that bite in the air, like stepping on the bathroom floor at four in

3

the morning. It ate at a man's bones, the cold, and damnit, he didn't like the cold, and that was that. No more winter, Johnny Lane has decreed, so winter is hereby abolished. That means no more mink coats, either. Wonder what all those high-stepping broads are gonna do without their mink coats. Probably freeze to death, even if it's summer all the time.

He looked up to the big apartment buildings on the other side of the park, and he wondered how it felt to live in one of those jobs, and wake up every morning and open the window and look out over the park instead of looking at some other guy in his undershirt opening the window and looking at you across the alleyway. The people from the apartment houses sometimes hit the spots, ooohing and ahhing, my, how quaint all this is. He'd seen them in their evening clothes, all dolled up, the women with dresses slashed to their navels, the men smoking pipes, like invaders from another world. They didn't belong in the neighborhood, and he resented them, but at the same time he envied the holiday spirit that was always with them.

And they call *us* the happy people, he thought bitterly.

He had been sitting on the bench for ten minutes when Snow White and the two cops pulled up. The white top of the squad car reflected the pale November sun, and it struck the old panic within him, but there was no place to go except deeper into the park, and that would be senseless. He sat still and wondered if he were carrying any mootah, but he remembered that he'd smoked his last joint down to a roach last night, and he was glad he wasn't hooked like some of the other cats, because these bastards would just be itching for a possession rap. He kept looking up at the apartment houses out there, far away on the other side of the park, pretending the cops weren't sitting in the car there at the curb, giving him the once-over. He heard the car doors slam shut with the solid sound of bank-vault doors, heard the empty clatter of the cops' shoes on the pavement, and then saw their shadows, long and thin in the afternoon sun, fall across the bench.

"Getting some air?" one cop asked.

He looked up, trying to feign surprise, knowing the fear was all over his face, and knowing cops could smell fear the way a hound could smell a bitch in heat. For an instant he panicked, thinking he *did* have a stick of marijuana on him after all. But he remembered that he had smoked it down, and the panic vanished.

"Yeah," he said, his voice trembling just a little. "I've been getting some air."

"We got a dead man," the second cop said dryly.

He blinked up at the cop, condemning himself for feeling guilty when he was completely innocent. But the neighborhood was one big festering guilt complex, and he was one ulcer in that sick system. He could not have felt innocent even if he'd wanted to.

"A dead man?" he said. "Yeah?"

"This is all news to you, huh?" the first cop said.

"Yeah. Yeah, it is."

"He got it with a zip gun, this guy," the cop went on. "You own a zip gun?"

"No," he said. He had owned a zip gun once, before the cops had begun giving the gangs a lot of trouble. He had ditched the gun together with a knife that was over the legal limit in blade length. He had been in street-gang fights since then, but he'd only used broken bottles or clubs, and sometimes he'd thrown bricks from the rooftops. But he'd never carried anything that could warrant a booking.

"You never owned one?" the cop asked.

"No, never," he lied.

"You know a guy called Luis?"

He knew instantly that it was Luis the Spic they were speaking of. He wet his lips. "Lots of guys named Luis," he said.

"Only one guy called Luis the Spic. You know him?"

5

"I know him," he said. "Sure. Everybody knows him."

"But you particularly, huh?"

"Why me, particularly?"

"Maybe because your name is Johnny Lane."

"That's my name," he said. "What's this all about?"

"Maybe because Luis tried to rape your girl say two or three weeks ago. Maybe, let's say, you and Luis had a big tangle outside the Apollo, with Luis pulling homemade brass knucks and trying to rip your face apart with them. Maybe that's why you know him particularly, huh, boy?"

"Luis tried to work over lots of guys. Everybody knows his brass knucks. He made 'em from a garbage-can handle. Besides, he's stayed away from me since that time near the Apollo. Luis don't bother me or my girl any more."

"You're right there, boy," the first cop said.

"What do you mean?"

"Luis ain't bothering *anybody* any more. It was Luis who got zip-gunned."

He wet his lips again. From up on Cathedral Parkway he heard a truck blasting its horn to the sky, high and strident. The blast hung on the silence of the November air, and he could almost taste the gasoline brackishness of the city. He sat still until the horn sound had dissolved, until all he could hear was the sound of muted traffic in the depths of the park, that and his own harsh breathing.

"I didn't shoot him," he said.

"I know," the first cop told him. "That's why you ran like a bastard when we came on the scene."

"Look," he said, appealing to their common sense now, "I didn't shoot him. I didn't like him, but there was lots of guys didn't like him." Their faces remained expressionless. "Look, why should I shoot him? I got plenty on my mind besides Luis the Spic."

"You're a big businessman," the second cop said wryly. "Lots of big deals on your mind."

6

"That ain't it, but . . . Hey, look, why would I want to shoot the bastard? Hey, come on now, you don't really think . . ."

He saw the look in the first cop's eyes. That same look was mirrored on the second cop's face. He saw, too, the irrefutable logic there. Luis the Spic had been gunned down. Luis was scum, but he was a citizen of this fair city. Someone had gunned the sonovabitch, and this was like tagging someone for a parking violation. Some big boy upstairs would raise six kinds of hell if this sort of thing went on, people cluttering up the streets with worthless garbage like Luis. First thing you knew, everyone would be leaving all their old gunned bodies around for the cops to clean up, and that would never do. There was only one way to handle a case of this exceptional caliber. Pull in the nearest sucker. Take Johnny, because he was as neat a patsy as the next guy, all made to order with an attempted rape on his girl, and a knock-down-drag-out right on 125th, where Luis had done his best to kill him. Pull in Johnny because all these tenement-crowded slobs were the same anyway, and if one of them fitted the bill, hang it on him.

He read the logic. He knew the logic, even if he didn't know it by name, because he'd read it in the eyes of cops ever since the days he used to swipe penny candies from Jake Soskovich on Lenox Avenue. Only this time it was homicide, and this time there wouldn't be a boot in the tail and a warning. People fried for homicide. Even when the dead man was a bastard like Luis.

You can't fight logic, but he tried to.

"Look," he said, "I mean it. Me and Luis was all squared away. I had no reason to—"

"Why'd you run?"

"What?"

"Why'd you run?"

"Hell, I didn't want no trouble with the cops. You know—"

7

"You got it now, boy," the first cop said.

"What're you wastin' time arguing with a nigger for?" the second cop said, and now the logic was clear and simple, and Johnny understood it perfectly this time. Because coupled with the logic was the warning "Remember last year," and last year was the year of the race riot, and the cops weren't taking any chances, nossir, not with zip guns in the picture. He read the logic like the writing on the wall, and this time he didn't try to fight it.

He brought his knee up into the groin of the first cop, and then clobbered him on the back of the head with both hands squeezed together like the head of a mallet. The cop fell to the pavement, and his buddy unsnapped the Police Special hanging in the holster near his right buttock. The shot rang out crisp and sharp, but Johnny was already behind the squad car, ducking around the grille, heading for the door near the driver's seat. He knew it was crazy, and he knew you didn't go around driving cops' cars, but taking the rap for Luis' kill was just as nuts, and he had nothing to lose now, not after the logic he had read.

He heard the second shot, and the third one, but he was already behind the wheel, his head ducked low, his hand releasing the emergency brake, his foot on the accelerator. The car leaped ahead, and then the shots came like bursts from a Tommy gun, fast and crackling, pinging against the sides of the car.

He heard the first cop banging his night stick against the pavement, and the pounding was as loud and as frightening as the bark of the other cop's gun. The last bullet found one of the rear tires, and the car lurched crazily, but he held onto the wheel and kept his foot pressed to the floor, and the rubber flapped and beat the asphalt as he headed crosstown. The cop had stopped to reload, and by the time the next shots came, he couldn't have hit the car if he'd been using a bazooka. He drove all the way down to Pleasant Avenue, wondering whether or not he should turn on

8

the siren, a little excited about all of it now, a little reckless-feeling.

He ditched the car, and then ran like a thief up to First Avenue, cutting back uptown. He reached 116th Street, wondered where he should go then. Back home? That was the first place they'd look. Cindy's? No, they'd look there, too.

He stood on the corner for a moment, looking over toward Third Avenue, wondering. When he saw a squad car pull around from Second Avenue, he made up his mind, and he made it up fast.

He didn't run this time. He walked casually, his head turned toward the shop windows that lined the street. He passed the big church, and then he passed the movie theatre west of Third Avenue, and he kept walking, unsure of himself because he was surrounded by whites, making sure he didn't look at any of the white women. He turned right on Lex, walking up toward 125th Street. On the corner of Lex and 125th, he looked back toward Third Avenue briefly, and then turned left, walking past the RKO Proctor's, past Park Avenue, past Madison Avenue and Mount Morris Park, past Fifth, penetrating deeper into Harlem.

He turned right again on Lenox Avenue, and now he was on his toes, watching for cops, because this was home ground and this was where they'd be looking. He walked cautiously. He tried to appear nonchalant, but his eyes raked each side street he passed, looking for the telltale white top of a squad car. There was a crowd in front of the synagogue on 128th, but there wasn't a cops' car in sight, so he figured it for a meeting or something. He kept walking uptown, looking west on 134th to the Y.M.C.A., and then to the Public Library on 135th.

He was in The Valley now, and he still didn't know where he should go because he didn't know where they would not look. He passed Harlem Hospital, and he wondered if this was where they'd taken Luis, and then he wondered if they took dead men to the hospital.

9

And abruptly he realized that Luis *was* dead, and that the cops thought he'd done it, and that he was a runaway.

He turned up 137th Street and headed for Seventh Avenue.

Chapter Two

The Corset Shop was on Seventh Avenue, between 137th and 138th. The plate-glass window carried the fancy legend "Foundation Garments," but everybody knew this was the Corset Shop, and everybody knew it was run by Gussie the Corset Lady.

He walked into the shop quickly. The front room was stacked with dummies wearing brassieres and girdles and corsets and contraptions he couldn't name. He'd worked for Gussie a long time ago, when he was fourteen, delivering the garments to fat women who should have ordered tents with zippers instead. He heard the hum of the sewing machine in the back room, and he looked out at the street once and then parted the flowered curtains and stepped out of sight.

Gussie looked up from the machine. She was a tall woman in her early fifties, with large brown eyes and full, sensuous lips. She was a warm tan color, and the Harlem rumble had it that she was from a rich family in the West Indies, but Gussie never called herself anything but "a nigger—and proud of it." She wore her own foundation garments, and she was wearing one now that bunched her full breasts up into the low yoke of her neckline, like the heroine on the jacket of a historical novel.

"Well!" she said. "Who's after *you?*"

"The cops," Johnny said quickly.

She'd been smiling, but the smile dropped from her face now, as if her little joke had paid off in unforeseen dividends. Her foot stopped on the treadle of the machine. "What d'you mean, the cops? What for?"

"They say I killed Luis the Spic."

11

"He dead?" Gussie asked. When he nodded she said, "Good. He deserved it."

"Yeah, but I didn't do it."

"I din't say you did. No matter who, he deserved it."

Johnny glanced through the curtains and out at the street again. "I run away from them," he said. "They was planning a run-through, and I don't like working on a railroad."

"You shouldn't have run, man," Gussie said. "That was stupid."

"All right, it was stupid. You didn't see their eyes."

Gussie stared at him contemplatively for a few moments. "Why'd you come to me?" she asked.

"Just to get off the streets. You don't have to worry. I'm leaving." He said it more bitterly than he'd intended to.

"I don't want no trouble with the bulls," she said lamely.

"Nobody does."

"Nor me especially."

Johnny forced a smile. "Hell, you pay the cops off regular, anyhow."

"That ain't got nothin' to do with it. I ain't askin' for trouble."

"You want me to go right this minute?"

"I din't say that."

"Then stop bellyaching."

Gussie's face was worried now. She was thinking hard, Johnny could see, and there was a phone on the wall not three feet from them. Maybe he shouldn't have come here after all. Maybe . . .

"What're y'gonna do?" she asked.

"I don't know. How do I know? Just stay away from them for now, that's all."

"And then what?"

"*Some*body killed Luis," he said. "That's for sure."

"They'll catch you," she said. "They'll catch you, an' you'll wisht you was back in Georgia, boy."

"I ain't from Georgia," Johnny said.

"You'll still wisht you was back there. Man, you

12

shun'ta run from them. That's the worst thing you could've done."

"I also slugged a cop and stole a pussy wagon. I got nothing to lose now."

"You're fixed up real fine, ain't you?" she asked.

"Yeah," he said dully.

They heard the front door open, and Johnny tensed. "Who . . ."

"Shut up," she hissed. "Stay back here. I'll take care of it."

He hugged the wall, and she parted the curtains and went out front.

"Afternoon, Gussie," he heard a woman's voice say.

"Afternoon, Mrs. Welles," Gussie answered. "Cold enough out there for you?"

"*Mm*-mmmmuh," Mrs. Welles said. "I come by to see if the corset was ready."

"It sure is, Mrs. Welles. Finished it this morning. Just a moment, now, an' I'll get it for you."

She parted the curtains again and came into the back of the shop. Johnny watched her as she checked the rows of cardboard boxes stacked on the long table. She selected one from the rest, turned, winked at him, and then went out front again.

"Here we are," she said heartily.

"Uh-huh," Mrs. Welles said, and Johnny could picture her nodding her head as she opened the box. "It looks very nice, Gussie, very nice. You mind if I try it on?"

"Well . . ." Gussie hesitated. "It's kind of chilly in the back. I don't want you catchin' pneumonia. You try it on home, and if there's anything to be changed, why, you just bring it right back. How's that?"

"Well, all right," Mrs. Welles said. She paused and then added, "If it's all right with you, Gussie, I'll pay you *after* I tries it on."

"Any time you're passing by," Gussie said agreeably.

"Don't know when that'll be," Mrs. Welles said. "Gettin' so a body's scared to walk the streets. You hear about Luis Ortega?"

"No," Gussie lied.

"Shot to death about an hour ago."

"No!" Gussie said.

"He was," Mrs. Welles said. "Serves him right, I say."

"Who shot him?" Gussie asked.

"Johnny Lane. You know Johnny Lane?"

"Well . . ."

"That's right, he used to work for you, didn't he? Well, him. He's the one. He shot Luis."

"Imagine that," Gussie said.

"Serves Luis right. I don't hold with no spics in Harlem, Gussie. Let 'em stay where they belong, I say."

"Well . . ."

"Besides, I give him enough of my money, that one. 'Tween us, Gussie, I think he was runnin' a crooked numbers game. Oh, I know they's folks say they hit from Luis, but I don't know of any personally, do you? I say it's good he got it."

"Have the police caught Johnny yet?" Gussie asked.

"I mind my own business when it comes to the cops," Mrs. Welles said. "They just itching for an excuse to pick you up on something." She paused and cleared her throat. "But I don't think they got him yet. Leastways, they took in his girl, Cynthia Matthews. You know her?"

"Yes, I know her," Gussie said slowly.

"Yeah, well, they got her down to headquarters. I guess they figure she may know something about it." Mrs. Welles sighed deeply. "I got to run home, Gussie. Now you sure this'll fit me?"

"Like a glove," Gussie promised.

"But will it fit like a corset?" Mrs. Welles asked, and then burst out laughing, convulsed by her own humor. She kept laughing until she walked out of the store, and Johnny relaxed only when he heard the door close. Gussie parted the curtains and stomped into the back room.

"That old bitch," she said. "I'll never see that money now."

"Why not?" Johnny asked.

"She won't come in again till this one's ready to fall off her bones. And by that time she'll have forgotten the bill. *Goddamn!*"

"Why'd you let her go, then?"

"Because she wanted to try the damn thing on. Suppose she'd come back here?"

"Oh," Johnny said.

"Yeah, oh."

"Look, I'll cut out," he said. "I don't want to cause you any—"

"Stay until dark," Gussie said suddenly. "Stay here in the back. When it gets dark, you can go."

"Thanks," he said.

"I'm only savin' my own skin. If the cops think—"

"Don't spoil it," Johnny said. "I was beginning to think you were human."

"Go to hell," Gussie said, but she was smiling.

She went back to the machine, and Johnny watched her as she set it in motion.

"I wonder what they're doing to Cindy," he said.

"Nothin'. Few questions, then they'll let her go."

"She don't know anything about it," he said.

"They'll let her go, don't worry."

"I ain't worryin'," he said. "They jus' *better* let her go."

"They will."

"This's just gonna kill Molly, you know that, don't you?"

"She'll survive," Gussie said. "Long as you din't shoot Luis, Molly'll get over it."

"I didn't shoot him," Johnny said.

"I know. So don't worry."

"You suppose they'll drag Molly into this, too?"

"I s'pose."

"Man, what gets me is I didn't do nothin'," Johnny said. "I mean, all this running, and—"

"Why don't you go to the cops?"

"You kidding?"

"If you din't shoot him—"

"I didn't."

"Then you got nothin' to be scared of."

"No, nothin'," Johnny said, pulling a face. "You think they care *who* shot that bastard? Long as their record's clean again, they don't give a damn."

"I s'pose," Gussie said philosophically. "Now shut up so I can get some work done."

He saw the lights come on in the shops across the avenue, saw the street lamps throw their feeble yellow rays into the gathering November darkness. The clock on the wall in Gussie's front room read five-ten. The lights all along the avenue were on now, building a solid cozy front against the crisp near-winter blackness.

"You'd better get started," she said. "We're lucky they haven't been here yet."

"I ditched the car on Pleasant," he told her. "They probably figure I'm mingling with the wops."

"Go through the back way," Gussie said. "You can cut through the yard and climb the fence. That way you'll come out on a Hun' thirty-eighth. Less lights."

"All right," he said. He hesitated, biting his lip.

"What's the matter?"

"Nothing."

"You scared?"

"A little."

"You got money?"

"A little."

Gussie walked to a chair and unhooked a black leather purse from where it hung. "This'll help a little," she said. "Things ain't been too good lately."

She handed him the sawbuck, and he hesitated before taking it. "You don't have to . . ."

"Luis broke my window once," she said simply.

"Well, thanks, Gussie. Thanks a lot."

She nodded, and he left by the back door, cutting into the concrete alleyway behind the apartment building. He avoided the garbage cans stacked for the night, walked alongside the wooden fence partitioning this house from the one alongside it. A woman up on the

16

fourth floor slammed open a window and put something on the fire escape. He huddled against the brick of the building until he heard the window go down again, and then he broke into a run. The clotheslines stretched overhead, flapping their garments like frozen ghosts. He reached the high green fence at the side of the house, scaled it, and dropped to the concrete on the other side. He ran through behind the house fronting on 138th Street, and then into the alley. He saw the garbage cans ahead. He knew there would be steps now leading to the sidewalk. He remembered the times when he and the other kids used to duck down behind the steps like this on his own block, whenever they were too busy or too rushed to look for a toilet.

He passed the garbage cans, and the familiar sharp stench assailed his nostrils. It was dark there where the steps dropped down into the bowels of the tenement. He saw the iron railing up ahead of him on the sidewalk, and the dangling chain that was supposed to stop kids from parading up and down the steps, but which only served as an impromptu swing. He started up the steps, and when he collided with the other man, he almost shrieked in terror.

He heard a dull clattering as something dropped to the steps and then rolled away into the blackness near the garbage cans. His fists balled immediately, and he waited, hearing the other man's hoarse breathing. He figured the guy for a wino or a stumblebum, or maybe a degenerate. He'd run across one when he was a kid once, scrambling down under the steps for bottle tops. He'd run like a bastard then, while the degenerate stood there with his clothes all open, cursing at him wildly.

"You sonovabitch," the man said. He could still not see his face. He heard only the hoarse breathing, saw only the dim outline of the man in the feeble glow of the street light that filtered down onto the steps below the building.

"Where'd it go?" the man asked.

"Where'd what go?" he heard himself answer.

17

"You sonovabitch," the man said again. He pushed past Johnny, dropped to his hands and knees, and began scrambling around near the garbage cans. Johnny looked at him for a moment and then thought, What the hell am I standing around for? He started up the steps, heard the sudden movement behind him, and then felt the wire fingers clamp onto his shoulder.

"Just a second, punk," the man said. "If you broke that goddamn syringe then you're going to pay for it." He pulled Johnny back down the steps, and Johnny stumbled and dropped to his knees.

"Just stick around," the man said. "You ain't going no place till we see the damage you done."

"Look, Mac . . ."

"Don't Mac me, bud. Just keep your mouth shut till I find that syringe. You think syringes grow on trees? I had to swipe this one from a doctor's bag."

Johnny got up and moved toward the steps again, and the man slammed him back against the wall. He was a big man, with arms like oaks and a head like a bullet. His eyes gleamed dully in the darkness. "I said stay where you are," he warned.

He shoved Johnny back into the alley, blocking him from the steps, and then he reached down for something that glittered near one of the garbage cans.

"You did it, you bastard," he said. "You broke the mother-lover." Johnny saw the jagged shards of the syringe in the man's open hand. And then the fingers of the hand closed around the syringe, hefting it like a knife, with the glass ends crooked and sharp.

"You shouldn't have been shooting up down here," Johnny said lamely. "I didn't even see you. I—"

"How much money you got, man?"

"Nothing," Johnny lied. He had the ten Gussie had given him, plus two of his own, but he sure as hell wasn't going to give it to a goddamn hophead with a broken hypo.

"Suppose we see," the man said, advancing with the broken shards of the syringe ahead of him.

Johnny lashed out with his right fist, catching the

man solidly on his chest. The man staggered back, raising the hand with the syringe high. The street light caught the syringe, gave it up to the darkness again as it slashed downward and up. Johnny felt the ragged glass ends when they struck his wrist. He tried to pull his hand back, but the biting glass followed his arm, ripping the thin sleeve of his coat, gouging through his Eisenhower jacket, the jacket his brother had brought home from the last war. The glass ripped skin clear to his elbow, and he felt the blood begin pouring down his arm, and he cursed the addict, and brought back his left hand balled at the same time, throwing it at the addict's head.

He felt his knuckles collide with the bridge of the bastard's nose, felt bone crush inward, and then the face fell away and back, slamming down against the concrete with the syringe shattering into a thousand brittle pieces now, now that it was too late. He stepped around the hophead, and the hophead moved, and Johnny kicked him in the left temple, wanting to knock his head clear off.

There was a pain in his arm, and the blood had soaked through the sleeves of his jacket and coat. He touched the arm and felt the blood, and when his hand came away sticky he felt a twinge of panic.

He stood at the base of the steps, wanting to kill the addict, really wanting to kill him. He had not felt this way even when he'd tangled with Luis that day outside the Apollo. It was one thing to be on the run, but it was another to have your arm all slashed to mincemeat, and he had the hophead to thank for that.

He kicked the bastard again, happy when he heard the sound of his shoe thudding against bone.

What do I do now? he wondered. How do I get through the streets with my arm running blood like this?

He needed a doctor, but a doctor was out. What about Cindy? No, not Cindy, because the cops would sure as hell be watching her now, especially after they picked her up for questioning. Goddamnit, how did I get into this? How, how . . . ?

No doctor, and no Cindy. What about a druggist? What about Frankie Parker, who worked for Old Man Lefkowitz? What about him? Did Frankie owe him a favor?

No, Frankie did not owe him a favor. But they'd grown up together, had lighted bonfires together on Election Eve, had thrown snowballs together, had roasted spuds together in the empty lot behind Davis' Grocery, had celebrated together every time Louis won a fight, had gone down to the Market together for the first time. Frankie owed him nothing, but what the hell, you grow up with a guy, you figure maybe a guy will do you that kind of a favor when your arm is running off into the gutter.

Maybe yes, and maybe no, but Frankie Parker was the only one to see, and Lefkowitz's drugstore was right on Seventh Avenue and only a few blocks down. He took his handkerchief from his pocket and wadded it into the sleeve of his jacket, near the elbow, where he figured it would stop the most blood. He looked down at the addict then, and he said, "You rotten bastard," and then he climbed the steps, straddled the chain, and stepped onto the sidewalk.

Chapter Three

The bell over the front door of the drugstore sounded loudly in the warm, antiseptic stillness.

Frankie Parker turned from the toiletries counter and saw Johnny entering the store, and he swallowed hard.

"Johnny!" he said, and then he lowered his voice and said, "Johnny," in a whisper, as if he were afraid of being overheard.

"Let's go in the back," Johnny said.

"Look, Johnny, you shouldn't have come here. The cops—"

"It's sure spreading fast, ain't it?" Johnny said. "Come on. In the back."

"Johnny, why'd you come here? You want to get me in trouble?"

"No, I don't want to get you in trouble," Johnny said wearily.

"Then why'd you come here? Man, you should've had more sense than that. Don't you know—"

"I want my arm bandaged. And something to stop the pain."

"What do you mean? What do you mean, you want . . ." Frankie looked at the bleeding arm, and then closed his eyes. He seemed about to get sick for a moment. He clutched the counter and asked, "How . . . how'd that happen? You . . . you kill somebody else, Johnny?"

"I ain't killed nobody yet. Look, Frankie, fix it for me, will you? You work in a drugstore, you know the ropes. Just a bandage, and something smeared on the cut, that's all."

"I'm not a doctor, Johnny. I'm only a pharmacist."

"You can fix it."

"Johnny . . ."

"You bastard, you'd better fix it," Johnny said tightly. "I'll rip your eyes out if you don't."

Frankie stared at him levelly. He bit his lower lip, and he wondered what Lefkowitz would do if he were here, and a sudden panic knifed his spine. Suppose Lefkowitz should come back?

"Come on in back," he said nervously. "Get out of the light, Johnny. For God's sake, the cops are looking all over for you."

"They still think I gunned Luis?"

"Didn't you?"

"You know damn well I didn't."

"I only know what I hear, Johnny."

They walked to the back of the shop, and Frankie led him to where the retorts and measures rested on a long brown table in one darkened corner. Johnny shrugged out of his coat, throwing it over the back of a chair. He rolled up the sleeve of his jacket, and he saw Frankie look sick again. Frankie touched the cut with probing, trembling fingers. The cut was a real bad one. It spread Johnny's arm in a jagged red streak.

"I . . . I . . ." Frankie tried to say something, and then wet his lips. There was a sheen of perspiration on his forehead now, and he blinked his eyes uncontrollably. "Johnny, why'd you have to come here? Did you have to come here?"

"Where else could I go? Could I go to a doctor?"

"No, but . . ."

"Where else? For Pete's sake, will you do something to stop the blood?"

"I . . . I will. I will," Frankie said wetting his lips again. He picked up a package of absorbent cotton, breaking the carton open with shaking hands.

"What're you so nervous about?" Johnny asked. "It's my goddamned arm."

"I know. I'm just . . . I wish you hadn't come here, Johnny." He fumbled with the blue paper, unrolled it, and ripped off a piece of cotton.

22

"Why? I told you I didn't kill Luis."

"Everybody says otherwise."

"Everybody's wrong then. Come on, fix my arm and I'll get the hell out of here."

"If you killed him, then I'm accessory after the fact by dressing your wound. You shouldn't have come here. I'm aiding and abetting—"

"Oh, shut the hell up!" Johnny said.

Frankie reached for a large bottle of peroxide and soaked the cotton with it. He put the cotton to the wound, and he saw Johnny's face tighten in pain.

"Easy, easy," Johnny said. "You trying to—"

"You've got to clean the wound," Frankie said. He ripped off another piece of cotton, and he was sweating freely now, and his eyes were narrowed. He was thinking of Andrea, the mulatto girl he'd met at a City College dance, and he was thinking of the drugstore he wanted to own one day. He worked on the cut methodically, unaware of Johnny's clenched fists and Johnny's tight mouth. He worked on the wound with the blood running red, but he did not think of the wound, he thought only that he was helping someone who was wanted by the police. He thought that, and the sweat rolled from his forehead and over the soggy collar of his shirt and down his back.

"I . . . I need some bandages," he said.

"All right, hurry it up," Johnny answered.

"Out front," Frankie said. He wet his lips and wiped the sweat from his forehead. "I . . . I keep them out front. I'll get some and come right back, Johnny."

"All right, go ahead."

"I'll be right back, Johnny," he said a little louder. "Don't move. The bleeding may stop if you don't move."

He went out front, and Johnny watched him go, and then he looked down at the cut. Damn if that addict hadn't done a dandy job on him, the sonovabitch. Well, Frankie would fix it. Frankie would bandage it, and at least he'd be able to walk the streets without leaving a trail of blood. He leaned back and looked at the walls of the room, at the bottles of pills and powders stacked on the shelves.

He waited for ten minutes, and finally Frankie came back, out of breath, still sweating.

"What the hell took so long?" Johnny asked.

"I . . . I had a customer."

"I didn't hear no bell," Johnny said.

"No? That's funny. It rang."

"You got the bandage?"

"Yes. Yes, here it is. Johnny, you really shouldn't have come here. I . . ."

"Is that the only song you know? Can't you see my arm is all cut up?"

"I'm sorry, Johnny, but I've got to think of myself, too. You can understand that, can't you?"

"All right, bandage my arm."

"But you can understand that, can't you? How a man has to think of himself, too? Is that being selfish, Johnny? A man has to think of his future, you know."

"What are you trying to tell me, Frankie?"

"Nothing."

"What are you sweating about?"

"What do you mean, sweating? I'm not sweating, Johnny."

"You're soaking wet." Johnny's eyes narrowed. "What took you so long out there, man?"

"Where, Johnny? Long out where?"

"Out front. Don't play dumb, Frankie. What took you so goddamn long?"

"I told you. I had a customer."

"What kind of customer?"

"A woman. A lady. She . . . she came in just as I went out front."

"What'd she buy?"

"What?"

Johnny jumped to his feet. "You heard me. What'd she buy?"

"Uh . . . a bottle of cough medicine."

"How come you didn't come back here for the pre-scription?"

"It's . . . Did I say cough medicine? I don't know what's wrong with me, Johnny. She bought milk of magnesia. She bought a—"

"Why didn't the bell over the door ring?"

"The bell? It did ring, Johnny. You just didn't hear it, that's all. The bell rang."

"Did you call the cops, you bastard?"

There was a moment of silence in the small room. The naked light bulb gleamed on the sweat clinging to Frankie's forehead.

"Did you?" Johnny shouted.

"A man has to think of himself, Johnny."

"You bastard," Johnny said. "Oh, you dirty—"

"What am I supposed to do? Throw everything over for you?"

The bell at the front of the store tinkled, and Johnny whirled suddenly. "Is that—"

"Back here!" Frankie screamed. "Back here, officers!"

Johnny froze. He seemed incapable of making a decision for a second, and then his head turned quickly, and he saw the door set in the side wall. He started for the door, remembered his coat, and turned back. He heard the footsteps runing for the back of the shop, and again seemed undecided for a fraction of an instant. He left the coat and ran for the door again, opening it and stepping outside. He was running before he hit the pavement.

He did not look back at his friend Frankie, nor did he hear what the cops said to him.

Chapter Four

The Grand is on 125th Street, just between Lexington and Third Avenues. It shows the movies the RKO Proctor's doesn't run, and it was there that Johnny went, taking a seat near the back, favoring his right arm by leaning over to the left and cradling the gashed wrist and forearm in his lap. He went there for two reasons. First, he went there because it was in Wop Harlem, and he did not think the cops would look for him there. Perhaps he should have gone downtown, to Times Square, maybe, but he didn't want to be too far away from the neighborhood in case the arm got really bad.

He went there, too, because he wanted time to think. The arm was beginning to hurt badly, and it wasn't easy to think now. Especially outside in the cold. He cursed Frankie again, and he wondered if he shouldn't have paused that extra moment, just long enough to pick up his overcoat.

He sat at the back of the theatre, the 3D glasses they had given him lying useless in his lap, alongside his cradled arm. Without the glasses, the screen was a distorted hodge-podge of color, but Johnny hadn't come here to catch up on the latest Hollywood attempt. He'd come to get a breather, come to figure a way out of the mess before it was too late.

The images on the screen did not help his thinking any. Like some nightmare world of demons, they flashed before his eyes, and he heard the sound and watched the kaleidoscopic colors, and lost himself in reliving the encounter with that sonovabitch addict who'd slashed him. He tried to figure, at the same time, just who'd killed Luis the Spic, but he came up with a list as long as his slashed arm. If Luis had anything, it had been a talent for making people dislike him.

The cops, of course, knew this. But they sought the best possible suspect, the one who'd had the best *recent* reason for killing Luis. If they had bothered to look more than ten inches beyond the tips of their dripping noses, they'd have realized that Luis was, among other things:

A dope pusher.

A bookie.

A pimp, on occasion.

A fence, on occasion.

A would-be rape artist, on occasion.

A bastard, always.

This was an impressive list when chalked up to a cat who was no more than twenty-eight years old, a most impressive list. And there were enough junkies, bettors, prostitutes and takers, petty jewel thieves and car-tire hijackers, outraged virgins and plain ordinary citizens who would have loved nothing better than to hold Luis' throat between their fingers while his eyes popped out of his goddamned skull and his tongue turned purple. Enough to fill the Grand on a Saturday—a rainy Saturday, at that. So the cops had reached into their bag and come up with Johnny Lane.

They had undoubtedly picked up his trail from Old Man Lefkowitz's. If he had another half hour here, he was good. And in a half hour, he had to figure it all out, and then start looking for the guy with the zip gun, because the only way the cops would ease off would be if he had the guy in tow.

Except, of course, that the gun was probably at the bottom of the Harlem River by this time.

And the guy was probably in Alaska or points west.

"You ain't even watching the picture," the girl said.

He turned abruptly, startled, ready to run. He thought at first that the girl was white, and he relaxed a little when he saw she was colored. She couldn't have been more than twenty. She wore a white sweater that was filled to capacity. He could see that even in the dark. She was pretty, he supposed, in a hard brassy way, with high cheekbones and full lips, blurred now by the darkness of the theatre. There was a vivid slash of lipstick across her mouth, and the whites of her eyes glowed in the reflection from the screen.

"No, I ain't," he said. He hadn't even noticed the girl sitting on his left, and he wondered now when she'd come in. She reeked of cheap perfume, but there was something exciting about the perfume and her nearness, and he tried to remember why the perfume stimulated him, but at the same time he told himself he had other things to think about besides some pickup in the movies.

"These three-D things are good," she said, taking the glasses from his lap, her hand brushing against his thigh. "Suppose to put these Hollywood women right in your arms. Don't you go for Hollywood women right in yours arms?"

"I . . . Look, I'm busy," he said.

"Too busy to watch the picture?"

He felt an instant panic. Had she heard about him? Did she know he was the one the cops wanted? What the hell was she doing in Wop Harlem, anyway?

"Yes," he said slowly, "too busy."

"Too busy for . . . other things, too?"

He caught the pitch then, and he remembered the perfume, the same cheap heady stuff he'd sniffed that time on the Market. An idea began kicking around in the back of his mind.

"Things like what?" he asked.

The girl sucked in a deep breath, and the sweater expanded in the darkness, high and full, straining. "Things like a way to kill the night. Better than doing eye-muscle tricks in a movie."

"How?" he asked.

"A room on Lex. Not the Waldorf, but clean sheets. A bottle, if you can afford it. Or a pipe. You choose your poison. Not to mention a price that's right."

"Like?" His mind was racing ahead now. A room on

Lex, away from the eyes of the cops, away from Nigger Harlem, more time to think, more time to work it all out.

"Like five for a roll," she said, "and seven-fifty for all night. Plus the bottle. You got seven-fifty?"

"I've got seven-fifty," he whispered.

"Don't let the price throw you, man. It's quality merchandise. I'm feeling generous."

"You're on," he said, making up his mind.

He saw her grin in the darkness. "I knew you was an intellectual," she said. "Come on."

They moved out of the row into the aisle, and she started for the rear of the theatre.

"This way," he said. "We'll use the exit down front."

"You ashamed or something?" she asked, her hands on her hips.

He decided to give it to her straight. "I got slashed in a fight. My arm is bleeding. I don't want to attract attention."

She stared at him for a few moments, and then said, "Long as only your arm is cut, that don't affect my business at all. Not at all."

They left the theatre, and he gave her the money for a jug, and then waited in the darkness of a hallway while she bought it in a brilliantly lighted liquor store. When she came back, she walked on the side of his wounded arm, blocking it effectively from inquisitive eyes.

"What are you doing so far east?" he asked her.

"How do you mean?"

"With the wops," he said.

The girl shrugged. "The *ofay* likes it black now and then." In Harlem, *ofay* was simply pig Latin for "foe."

"And do you like it white?" he asked suspiciously.

"Business is business," she said.

"You ever operate in Harlem? *Our* Harlem?"

"No."

"Why not?"

"I got my reasons. Listen, who're you, the D.A.? Do you want this, or don't you?"

"I want it," he said, thinking, I only want the room, baby. You can stuff the rest.

They walked in silence to a brownstone set next to a delicatessen. She led him up the steps and opened the wooden door to her room. It was a small room, with a bare bulb hanging overhead and a dresser in one corner. A bed occupied most of the room, and there was a table with an enamel washbasin on a stand alongside the bed.

"Like I said," she told him, "it ain't the Waldorf."

She was not as big as he'd thought she was in the movies. She was, in fact, almost small except for the breasts that crowded the woolen sweater. He unconsciously compared her to Cindy in his mind, and his eyes roamed her body candidly. She saw his eyes on her and said, "Look O.K.?"

"Looks fine," he answered. He could not manage a smile.

"Which shall we treat first? The arm or the gullet or whatever?"

"Have a drink, if you want," he said. "I can wait."

"Yeah, but you're bleeding on my imported Persian rug." She grinned and went to the dresser, taking out a bottle of peroxide and a roll of gauze.

"I already had the peroxide treatment," he said bitterly.

"Little more won't hurt." She led him to the basin, took off his jacket, and then rolled up the sleeve of his shirt. "Besides," she said, "don't kick about the service. You'd never get this on the Market."

"Don't I know it," he said.

She studied the cut more closely. "You run into a buzz saw?"

"No, a hophead."

"Same thing," she said, pouring the peroxide onto the wound. He winced, holding back the scream that bubbled onto his lips.

"You got glass in there."

"Pull it out, if you can."

She looked at him curiously. "Sure," she said. She

wrapped absorbent cotton around a toothpick, and then began fishing for the glass splinters. Each time she got one, he clamped his teeth down hard, and finally it was all over. She drenched the arm in peroxide again, and then wrapped the gauze around it, so tight that he could feel the veins throbbing against the thin material.

"That rates a swallow," she said. She broke the seal on the fifth, poured whisky for them both into water glasses, and handed him one. "Here's to the hophead," she said.

"May he drop dead," Johnny answered, tossing off the drink. It burned a hole clear down to his stomach, and he remembered abruptly that he hadn't eaten for a good long while.

The girl took another drink, and then put the glass and the bottle on the dresser top again. "Well, now," she said. "Let's try to forget that arm, shall we?"

She moved closer to him, and he thought of Cindy and of his real reasons for coming up here. "Look . . ." he started.

The sweater moved in on him, warm and high, soft, beating with the soft muted beat of her heart beneath the wool and the flesh. He tried to move away, but she took the back of his head and pressed his face tight against the wool. He sat on the edge of the bed, and she stood in front of him, and he thought, Cindy, Cindy, and then he thought, I'm tired, I'm goddamn tired, and then he thought, The hell with Cindy, the hell with the cops, the hell with Luis, the hell with everyone. His hands dropped behind her, seizing the thin silk of her skirt, tightening there fiercely.

"Say, easy now, man," she said, chiding, smiling. "Easy now. Slow and easy."

She stepped back from him, dipped her head, and reached her arms up suddenly. The white sweater slid up over smooth brown skin. She pulled it over her head, and then threw her shoulders back, proud of what she'd uncovered, watching his face and watching him wet his lips and suck in a deep breath, and smiling

31

all the while because this was her trade and she knew she was good at her trade.

She took a step closer to him, a sad, wise, happy, unhappy smile on her face. "Now, don't break me, man," she said. "Nice and easy now, you promise?"

She took the back of his head again, and her fingers toyed with his hair. She kissed his nose, and his mouth, and his ears, and when his hands tightened on her again, she caught his wrists and held them away from her.

"You promised, now," she scolded, enjoying his eagerness. "Besides, you have a bad arm."

And then she kissed him soundly, with her body molded firmly to his, and she let his hands go wild this time, and the knock sounded on the door.

She broke away from him, and he leaped to his feet.

"Who . . ." he whispered.

"Shut up. Get in the closet. Quick."

He went to the closet, feeling foolish as hell, feeling like the jackass in some low comedy of errors. The closet door closed on him, leaving him in darkness, leaving him with trailing silk dresses flapping around his face, high-heeled shoes crushed under his big feet. The smell of the cheap perfume was strong in the closet, and he could not stop feeling foolish. He heard the outside door open, and then the man's voice.

"What took you so long, Ada?"

"Oh, hello, Tony. I was—taking a nap."

Why did she say that? Why didn't she say, "I've got someone with me, Tony. Come back later, come back in the morning"? Why the song and dance?

"Taking a nap, huh?" The voice was a big voice. It belonged to a big man. It belonged to a suspicious man. Johnny did not like that voice, and the voice was in the room now, moving in from the outside door.

"What's this?" the voice asked.

"What's what, Tony?"

"This jacket. You wearing Army jackets now, Ada? That what you doing?"

"Tony . . ."

"Shut up! Just shut up! Where is he?"

"Where's who? Tony, I was just taking a nap. The jacket belongs to a fellow came to fix the plumbing. He must have left it here. The plumbing leaked. He—"

"Did the plumbing leak blood? Did it leak blood in that basin there? I'm going to break that sonovabitch's head in two! Where is he?"

"I told you, Tony. There's no one."

"And I told you! I told you what would happen if I caught you up to your old tricks again. Where is he?"

The footsteps were advancing across the room now, and it was a cinch Tony would look in the closet first. His voice was the voice of a man who couldn't be talked to, and whereas Johnny couldn't understand all this concern over a common whore, he didn't stop to ponder it too deeply. He dropped to his knees quickly, rooting around on the closet floor for a shoe. He found a sturdy-feeling job with a spike heel, and he got to his feet again and waited, clutching the shoe tightly around its instep.

"You got him in the closet?" the voice asked, close now. And then the door opened on Johnny, and the shaft of light spilled onto his face. He didn't hesitate an instant. He brought the shoe up and then down in a fast motion, catching Tony on the bridge of his nose.

Tony was big, all right, big and bearded, wearing a leather jacket and corduroy slacks. A from-nowhere joe, but he was big, and the bigness counted right now. The shoe caught him on his nose, and the line of blood appeared magically, and then he stumbled backward. Johnny swung out with his left hand, catching Tony in the gut. He hit him again with the shoe, and as Tony went down, he heard the girl screaming, screaming, her voice like a busted air-raid siren.

"You bastard!" she shrieked. "You filthy bastard! He's my brother! He's my brother!"

He ran down the steps and out into the street, a little sorry Tony had arrived when he had, and a little sorry he'd left an almost full fifth of good whisky in the room.

The fifth had cost him close to four bucks. Well, he'd got a bandage for his arm out of it, if nothing else.

It didn't seem to matter, at the moment, that blood was already beginning to seep through that bandage.

Chapter Five

Detective First/Grade Leo Palazzo lived on 218th Street between Bronxwood and Paulding Avenues. He had always liked that Olinville section of the Bronx until recently, and he had only begun to dislike it when Negroes started drifting into the neighborhood. He was now considering a house out in Babylon, where $2,400 down would give him something he could call his own—provided he could get out of the city system and establish himself on the Island.

He had been a cop for a long time, and he was, by certain standards, a good cop. He would not think of leaving the force, and unless the Suffolk County police had an open detective's chair for him, he would stay right where he was. Palazzo worked in Harlem.

He was holding in his hands now a telephone message that had been clocked in at 7:33. The message told him that a liquor store on Lenox and 129th had been held up by two masked men driving a Chevrolet sedan. The message had already been broadcast to the RMP cars in the vicinity, and Car 21 had been dispatched to the scene of the crime, awaiting Detectives Donnelly and O'Brien, who were on their way. Palazzo looked at the message briefly, not because it concerned him, but because he liked to know a little bit of everything that went on in the precinct. He had long since reached the conclusion that the Skipper was an incompetent old man who'd been tossed the precinct as a political plum. In Palazzo's mind, there was one cop who rightfully deserved to command here, and that cop was Detective First/Grade Leo Palazzo. So he kept his thumb in every pie, watching, waiting, consoling himself with the thought that the Suffolk County police would know what to do with a man of his caliber.

He threw the message on the desk and said, "That's all they know how to do. Steal and screw."

Dave Trachetti looked up from his third cup of coffee since supper. In contrast to Palazzo, he was a thin man, with receding hair and a long, hawklike nose. Palazzo's bigness sometimes annoyed Trachetti. No man had a right to be that big. It made anyone around him feel ill at ease.

"You're maladjusted, Leo," Trachetti said.

"Don't I know it, friend," Palazzo answered. "I should have been a personal bodyguard to some rich society broad."

"You should have been something, that's for sure."

Palazzo grinned, allowing himself the luxury of a moment of humor. He turned all business then. "Who's this punk you've got?"

"His name is Brown," Trachetti said. "We had him in here twice before on holding charges, second time with intent to sell. He used to run a small-potatoes shooting gallery, but we busted that up last May."

"Is he still pushing?"

"I don't think so, Leo. Leastwise, not according to the rumble. He's on C, though. Had a bindle on him when we picked him up, and he's about ready to claw down the walls now."

"Let him claw," Palazzo said. "These goddamn junkies . . ."

"Sure, but that's not why I wanted you to talk to him, Leo."

"Why, then?"

"He was heeled when we picked him up. A zip gun, Leo."

"Yeah?" Palazzo said, showing his first sign of interest.

"He started a fight in one of the bars, and Klein hauled him in. He was hopped and didn't know what the hell was going on until just a little while ago. He wants to see a lawyer."

"A lawyer," Palazzo said disgustedly. "These punks all act as if they're top man in the rackets. A lawyer!" He shook his head, and his face looked as if he were ready to spit. "Where is he?"

"I got him in Interrogation. I mean, Leo, we should dump him if all it amounts to is a bar brawl. But I thought the zip gun might interest you. Seeing as how you're working on the Ortega kill."

"That's all cut and dried," Palazzo said. "But I'll talk to this punk, anyway. You want to come along?"

"Mary ought to be calling in soon," Trachetti said.

"Boy, she's really got you wrapped, hasn't she?" Palazzo paused. "Tell me, Dave, haven't you ever been tempted by any of this high-yellow stuff we get in here?"

"Nope," Trachetti said lightly.

"I figured. You've got no blood, that's all. Don't you know it's good for a change of luck, Dave?"

"My luck's been all right so far," Trachetti answered.

"Yeah." Palazzo shrugged. "I'll be in Interrogation if anybody wants me." He left the squad room and walked down the corridor to Interrogation. He stopped to talk to the uniformed patrolman outside the door, and then walked into the room. Brown was sitting in a straight-backed chair near the desk. He did not look up.

"Your name Brown?" Palazzo asked from the door.

"Yeah," Brown answered.

Palazzo closed the door and walked over to the desk. "What's your first name, punk?" he asked.

"Charles," Brown said. He was a small Negro with the sunken, hollow eyes of an addict. His hands twisted nervously in his lap now, and he could not control the tic at the corner of his thin mouth.

"All right, Charlie, what's it all about?"

"Man gets in a little scrap, ain't no reason to make it a federal case," Brown said.

"I understand you're on C," Palazzo said.

"Who told you that? Man, the dreams you guys can build!"

"Look, Charlie, let's cut the crap. We had you in here twice before, both times on narcotics offenses. We also busted the private shooting gallery you were running on Park Avenue. So don't give me any horse manure, Charlie. I'm not the guy to play games with."

"I don't know what you're talking about," Brown said. "Maybe I used to shoot up a little, but I don't no more. Man, C is for the birds."

"You selling the stuff, Charlie?"

"What stuff, man?"

"Charlie," Palazzo said tightly, "I don't go for smart guys. The sooner we get that straight, the better off you'll be. Answer my questions and answer them straight. Are you selling the stuff?"

"What stuff?" Brown asked.

Palazzo brought back his hand suddenly, and then lashed out at Brown with an open palm. He caught Brown just below the left eye, and Brown's head twisted to one side, and then his eyes narrowed in hate. "I want a lawyer," he said.

"You'll get one if you need one. Are you selling the stuff?"

"No," Brown said.

"But you are a user."

"I don't know what you mean," Brown said.

Palazzo slapped him again, harder this time. He leaned over Brown and said, "This can get as rough as you want it, pal. Are you a user?"

"Yes."

"Cocaine?"

"Yes."

"Who supplies you?"

"Different people. Hell, you know all the pushers. What're you jumpin' on me for?"

"Why'd you start that fight in the bar?"

"Some guy said something I didn't like."

"What'd he say?"

"I don't remember. I was stoned." Brown sucked in

a deep breath of air. "Look, that bindle you guys lifted from me. I mean, how about it? You don't want a man to get sick all over the floor, do you?"

"You get sick, and you'll wipe it up, Charlie."

"Look," Brown said, "I been meanin' to go to Lexington, no foolin'. I know guys who been there, and they shake the monkey one-two-six. You let me have that bindle, and I fly for Kentucky first thing. Whattaya say?"

"I say you're full of crap, Charlie."

"No, no, I'm tellin' the truth, Lieutenant. I—"

"Detective," Palazzo corrected.

"Yeah, well, I'm tellin' the truth. I been plannin' on goin' down there all along. But let me have the bindle now, and then I'll get a little pile of stuff to hold me till I get down there, that's all. Come on, Lieutenant, we can forget that fight in the bar, can't we?"

"Maybe. But maybe we can't forget the zip gun."

"What . . . what zip gun?" Brown asked.

"The zip gun," Palazzo said, smiling. "You know, Charlie, a zip gun. A hunk of pipe with a homemade firing pin and a wooden handle. Zip gun, Charlie. Ring a bell, Charlie?"

"I never owned a gun in my life," Brown said, shaking his head. "You must be mistaken, Lieutenant."

"Knock off that 'Lieutenant' crap," Palazzo said angrily. "We took the zip gun from you when we booked you. You were so blind you didn't know what the hell was going on. What were you doing with a zip gun, Brown?"

"This is all news to me, sir," Brown said. "I'm tellin' you—"

"And I'm telling you we can play this as rough as you like. Don't try denying things we already know. The zip gun was in your pocket, Brown."

"All right, maybe I had a gun."

"What were you doing with it?"

"Well, you know Harlem, man. A fellow needs some kind of protection, don't he?"

"Who supplied you, Charlie?"

39

"Suppl— Oh, you mean the stuff." He seemed relieved to be getting away from the topic of the zip gun. "Lots of guys."

"Andy Barron?"

"Who's he?"

"You know who he is. Did you ever take from him?"

"Sometimes, I think. Man, you get it where you can."

"What about Ortega?"

"Who?"

"Luis Ortega."

"I don't think I know him," Brown said.

"Everybody in Harlem knows him, Charlie. Luis the Spic. Luis Ortega. Do you recall his name now?"

"Oh, yes," Brown said, "I think I do. Luis the Spic. Yes, I seen him around now and then."

"You ever take from him?"

"Man, I didn't even know he was pushin'."

Palazzo brought back his hand and threw it at Brown's head, balled this time. Brown's head snapped backward, and then he blinked his eyes.

"Don't lie to me, Charlie. Whatever you do, don't lie to me. You know damn well Luis was pushing."

"All right, I knew it," Brown said sullenly.

"You ever take from him?"

"Once or twice."

"Recently?"

"No."

"Why not?"

"I just didn't. Is there a law says where a man has to get his fix?"

"No, but there's a law against killing people," Palazzo said.

"Well, that don't apply to me. I ain't killed nobody."

"The Ballistics boys tell me your gun was fired recently, Charlie," Palazzo lied. "How about that?"

"They must be mistaken, man," Brown said.

"They don't make mistakes, Charlie. Never. If they say it was fired, it was fired. Who'd you shoot it at?"

"Me? Man, I ain't shot that thing since I picked it up."

"Then who did fire it?"

"Search me." Brown shook his head." Beats me, sir."

"When's the last time you saw Luis?"

"The Spic, you mean? Hell, I don't know. Must be months now."

"Where were you this afternoon at about three-thirty?"

"Three-thirty? Well, now, lemme see."

"Come on, Charlie."

"I think I was home. Sleepin'."

"Anybody home with you?"

"No, I don't think so."

"Anyone see you between three and five, Charlie?"

"Well, now, I don't think so."

"Your gun was fired at about three-fifteen." Palazzo lied again. "That's what Ballistics says. What do *you* say, Charlie?"

"They must be mistaken," Brown answered.

"I told you they don't make mistakes. Where'd you shoot that gun?"

"I didn't shoo—"

Palazzo grabbed Brown's collar with one hand, and he brought his other fist forward with full force so that it collided with Brown's mouth. A splash of blood stained Brown's teeth, and he spat onto the floor and said, "You won't get away with this, you know. I know my rights."

"Where'd you shoot that gun?" Palazzo asked, holding on to Brown's collar.

"I told you—"

Palazzo hit him again. Brown slumped in the chair, and Palazzo yanked him erect again.

"Where'd you shoot the gun?"

"I didn't—"

Again Palazzo hit him, and a dull glaze came into Brown's eyes. He almost fell off the chair, but Palazzo held him tightly.

41

"We can use a hose, Brown," he said. "Where'd you shoot the gun?"

"From my window," Brown said suddenly.

"At who?"

"At a cat. A cat out there was makin' a racket. I shot at him."

"You're a liar, Brown."

"I shot at a cat," Brown insisted.

"A cat named Luis."

"I don't know the cat's name," Brown said. "I just shot 'cause he was meowin'."

"What happened, Brown? Wouldn't he fix you? Was that it?"

"Wouldn't who fix me?"

"All right, you bastard," Palazzo said. "All right, Charlie, we play it your way." He stepped back from Brown and took off his jacket, and then he began rolling up his shirt sleeves. His barrel chest heaved as he worked, and the butt of his .38 bobbed in its shoulder holster. He walked over to Brown then and lifted him from the chair, holding his jacket front in both big hands.

"Tell me you shot Luis, Charlie. Tell me all about it."

"I shot at a cat," Brown insisted.

Palazzo shoved him away suddenly, and Brown whirled back across the room and collided with the wall. He got to his feet, and Palazzo was on him instantly.

"You shot Luis, didn't you?"

"No."

Palazzo brought his knee up into Brown's groin, and Brown screamed in pain and terror.

"You shot him," Palazzo said.

"No! No!"

Palazzo drove his big fist into Brown's gut, and when Brown bent over he gave him the flat edge of his hand on the back of his neck. Brown fell forward on his face, and Palazzo kicked him in the ribs.

"This is just the beginning, black boy," he said, and

maybe it was those words that changed Brown's mind. Palazzo reached down for him and propped him up against the wall, bringing back his fist again.

"All right," Brown said wearily.

"You shot him?"

"I shot him."

"Stenographer!" Palazzo yelled. He waited until he heard footsteps in the corridor outside, and then he said, "All right, Charlie, now you can tell us all about it."

It was amazing the way Brown loosened up once the stenographer was there to take down the information. He almost seemed proud of his shooting prowess. He told them how he'd gone to Luis for a fix, and how Luis had refused him because he didn't have a fiver. He'd offered Luis two, but Luis had remained adamant, and finally Brown had threatened him with the zip gun. Luis had laughed in his face, and that was the last time Luis laughed at anything. The stenographer took all this down, and then Brown signed it in a scrawling hand and asked, "Can I have that bindle now?" and Palazzo had just laughed and left the room with the signed confession in his mitts. And that had been that.

Except for Johnny Lane.

"What about the other guy?" Trachetti asked Palazzo.

"What other guy?" Palazzo asked.

"The one slugged March and swiped the RMP. Him."

"Screw him," Palazzo said. "He's clean now, ain't he?"

"Yeah." Trachetti paused. "So what happens to him now?"

"How the hell do I know? The word'll get around, I suppose, sooner or later. When he knows the heat's off, he'll come out in the open again."

Trachetti wiped a hand over his face. "What I mean, Leo, shouldn't we wise the kid up? You know, he still thinks he's got a murder rap hanging over his head."

"So what?" Palazzo asked.

"Well, hell, he's out there someplace thinking—"

"Who cares what the hell he's thinking? He probably done something anyway, the way he ran."

"Still . . ."

"You're too damn softhearted. You think we're working up in Larchmont or New Rochelle or someplace. Well, we ain't. This is Harlem. This is where cops get their throats slit. You think any of these bastards is worrying about us? Well, they ain't, I can tell you that. You want me to go out and look for this other guy, whatever the hell his name is? Tell him he's clear, pat him on the head, kiss him on the cheek? He'd probably knife me if I got within ten feet of him."

"I don't think so," Trachetti said. "Couldn't we at least tell his family? Or the girl?"

"Ah-ha, so that's it. You just want another look at his broad, eh, Dave? She was a piece, I got to admit that."

"Aw, come on, Leo, don't be stupid. That kid—"

"I don't give a damn about that kid," Palazzo said, almost shouting. "Let him find out the good news by himself. Serve him right for slugging March and swiping the car."

"Suppose he does something else? He thinks he's wanted for murder, Leo, don't you understand?"

"He'll live," Palazzo said. "He's healthy, ain't he? He's young. He's sound of mind and body. From the way March tells me he ran, he must be a hardy specimen."

"A murder rap . . ." Trachetti started.

"Murder rap, shmurder rap," Palazzo cracked. "So long as you got your health."

Chapter Six

The arm began bleeding in earnest again.

It started as a slow trickle of blood that oozed its way through the fresh bandage. But the trickle became a stream, and the stream soaked through the bandage and dripped onto Johnny's wrist, and the drops ran into his cupped palm, hung on his fingertips, and then spattered onto the sidewalk in a crimson trail.

It got colder, too, and he missed his jacket, and he cursed himself for not having grabbed it when he'd left the girl's room. With her screaming like that, though, it's a wonder he'd managed to remember his head, even. Still, it was goddamn cold, too cold for November, too cold even for January.

He marveled at the way the blood flowed. He watched it with a curious detachment, and he wondered if he weren't getting delirious. The blood rushed out of his arm with a peculiar urgency. It was almost as if the body were screaming, screaming a vivid red.

I have to stop the blood, he thought. If I don't stop the blood, I'll die.

The thought of dying had not occurred to him before. He had been concerned with only one thing before, and that was avoiding the police. He'd wanted to dress the arm, too, but that was a secondary consideration. He thought of dying now, and the thought did not particularly frighten him. He examined the thought with detachment, the same way he'd looked at his arm. He did not want to die, but somehow it didn't seem important to him, one way or the other.

But I have to stop the bleeding, he told himself. I'm beginning to feel weak already, but maybe that's because I'm hungry. When did I eat last? I'm cold, I wish

I had a coat. I have to stop the blood. The police . . .

He suddenly got rattled. He seemed incapable of thinking clearly for a few moments. He shook his head, trying to clear it, and he found himself trembling, and he realized he was scared, scared stiff, and then he thought of dying again, and this time the thought frightened him. His teeth chattered, and he tried to think clearly, tried to get all the thoughts in order, tried to arrange them neatly. But there was only a kind of screaming inside his head, a lonesome grating plea to someone, anyone, anything to stop the blood and the running and the cold.

He alternately shook his head and nodded it. He stared around him, almost dazed, completely overwhelmed by the thoughts that bombarded his brain.

He bit down on his lip then, hard, feeling the pain, almost drawing fresh blood. He stared at a spot in the concrete, trembling, waiting for the tremor to leave his body, waiting for his head to clear.

How do you stop bleeding? he asked himself. Goddamnit, how do you stop bleeding?

A tourniquet.

Yes, a tourniquet. You make a tourniquet. You use a rag and a stick and a hank of hair. You tighten it all around your arm, and you mutter mumbo-jumbo, and the bleeding stops magically.

How do you spell tourniquet? he wondered, his mind wandering.

You spell it with a rag and a stick and a hank of hair. I haven't got a handkerchief any more, but I can tear my shirt. It's an old shirt, anyway. I can tear it. I can tear it if I've got the strength to tear it. I can tear it down where it sticks into my pants, where nobody will see it. Then I need a stick and the hank of hair, that was a joke. You understand, a joke. Something to laugh at. I don't really need a hank of hair, I just need a stick.

He had a purpose now. He had to find a stick.

How many sticks are there in The Valley?

Millions. All kinds of sticks. A stick of marijuana. A

matchstick, and a lipstick, but all I need is a stick to turn the rag with.

His eyes scoured the pavement and the gutter. He stopped at every garbage can he passed, and he thought, Man, where are all the sticks tonight?

He began to tremble again, and the panic followed the trembling.

God, he thought, just give me a little stick. I'll forget the Caddy. I don't want the Caddy. I can't use a Caddy on a tourniquet. All I want is a stick. Is that too much? his mind screamed. Is that too much to ask? Just a goddamned stick, only a stick for my arm, can't I have a stick, please, not even that, just that, please, please?

He found himself crying. He had not cried since he was thirteen and Molly found him with a girl in the apartment. He wasn't doing anything with the girl, even, oh, maybe a little feel, she was only a kid, too. But Molly had popped in, and the girl—he couldn't even remember her name—had tried to button up her blouse, and he could remember her long, thin fingers fumbling with the buttons now, and her small breasts quivering. And Molly had started screaming and chased the girl out, and then she'd beat him with a stick, and oh, Lord, he wished he had that stick now. He would kiss Molly's hands and let her beat him all she wanted if he could only have that stick now. And as he thought of the stick, and of Molly, and of that girl long ago whose name he didn't even remember, the tears came stronger, and he felt certain he was going to die now.

He almost passed the orange crate by. It was stacked alongside one of the garbage cans, and there was an oily paper bag in it, and some of the dripping from the bag had spilled over onto the bottom of the crate. He spotted the crate through blurred eyes, and he wiped the back of his hand across his eyes and reached down for the box. The blood from his arm dripped in a steady tattoo on the thin wood, and he watched the way the wood absorbed the blood, the way the blood stained the wood and magically brought out its grain. He knew orange crates well. He knew how to take them apart expertly. You had to take an orange crate apart to get at the strong frame on either end of it. And you had to have those frames if you wanted to make rubber-band guns for shooting linoleum squares. He had almost blinded his best friend with a linoleum square snapped from a rubber-band gun a long time ago. The kid had moved, shortly after that, up to the Bronx, but Johnny had never forgotten the time he almost blinded him.

He didn't need the hard frame of the orange crate now. All he needed was one of the slender slats, and he broke that off quickly, and then ran with it, as if he'd lifted a piece of jewelry or a purse. He found a dim hallway, and he went to the back of the building and crouched behind the steps, pulling his shirt out of his pants. He caught the material between his teeth, tasting the fabric, starting the tear. He tore it all the way with his hands then, having to tug harder where the seam was joined.

He didn't know quite where to put the tourniquet. He tried it just above the elbow, hoping to cut off the blood supply that way. He wrapped the cloth around his arm, and then he tangled it around the stick and started tightening it. He turned the stick like the handle of a vise, and he felt the pressure above his elbow, and he kept tightening, wondering if his arm would fall off when the blood stopped. He watched the stream of blood. He watched it with the careful scrutiny of a microbe hunter. It seemed to be letting up.

Yes, it was letting up. It wasn't bleeding so badly now. He held the stick tightly in his left hand, not allowing it to loosen. When the blood stopped completely, he almost started crying again. Man, he thought, this is the longest crying jag I've ever been on. But he felt a sudden peace inside him when the blood stopped, and he sighed thankfully.

Come on, blood, he thought, clot.

He held the stick for a long while, waiting for the

blood to clot. He had no conception of time any more. Time was for people who had to be home for supper, for people who had to meet other people, for people who had to get up for work in the morning. He had no need for time.

When he thought the blood had clotted, he released the stick, slowly, very slowly, almost expecting the flow of blood to start again. It did not start. He tied a makeshift bandage around the wound, tearing off another piece of his shirt. He broke the stick and put half of it in his back pocket, in case he needed another tourniquet. He felt better, a whole lot better.

He'd solved one of the problems; he'd stopped the blood. Now he needed something to eat. A place to rest. An overcoat. He sure as hell needed an overcoat. He wouldn't bleed to death now, but he might very well freeze to death.

One thing at a time, he told himself. No more confusion now. One thing at a time. Take a place to rest, something to eat, and an overcoat. Roll them all into one big ball, and what do you get? Help. He needed someone to help him. Molly? Cindy?

The cops had already questioned Cindy. Maybe she was the best bet. He'd have to try it, anyway.

He left the hallway and began scouting for a phone booth. It was funny how nobody looked at him. It was cold as a bastard, and he was walking around in his shirt sleeves, and nobody gave him a second glance. What a goddamn rotten world, he figured. Everybody so wrapped up in what they were doing, they didn't give two hoots about somebody in his shirt sleeves when it was so cold out. Well, that was to his advantage. Let them be all wrapped up in what they were doing. If they took a second look at his shirt, they'd take a second look at his arm. He didn't want that.

So how was he going to get into a phone booth without someone spotting that arm? Hell, why did everything have to be so difficult? A simple thing like making a goddamn phone call! You make a phone call by walking into a booth and dialing. You don't go around working out a strategy. That's plain stupid. Well, it may be stupid, boy, but you got to do it. Have you got a dime?

He fished into his pocket, pulling out the change there, the task made difficult because he kept his change in his right pocket, and he wasn't using his right arm at the moment. He twisted his left arm until he got the change, and then he jiggled it on his palm and studied it. Four pennies. A quarter. A fifty-cent piece. A subway token. A nickel.

No dime.

He wasn't surprised. The way things were going for him, he was lucky he had any change at all. But no dime, and that meant he'd have to make change, and that meant the risk of having the arm spotted.

Now wait a minute, don't start panicking again. Man, you're the most berserk-running cat in Harlem. Just take it easy. You think things out, and they're all easy that way. Like who says you have to get change at the cigar counter or the drug counter or whatever counter you stop to make the call? Is there a law says that? Why can't you stop at one of the newsstands outside the subway? Why can't you stop there, show the newsstand keeper your left side, hell, find one run by a blind man, even? Let's start using that head, man, or we're gonna wind up behind the eight ball.

He walked to the nearest subway station, his shoulders hunched against the cold. He tucked his right hand into his pocket. He walked quickly, and he felt the cold biting at his skin. His ears were particularly cold. His ears and his feet, and when your ears and feet are cold, you feel cold all over.

The newsstand on the west side of the avenue, squatting near the subway entrance there, was closed. He cursed silently and crossed the street, a smile mushrooming onto his face when he saw that the newsstand there was open. He walked to the stand quickly.

He picked up a copy of the New York Post, plunked down the quarter, and waited for his change. He stood with his left side toward the stand, hiding his bloody right arm. The news dealer put down a dime and a nickel on a stack of Amsterdam Newses. Johnny said nothing. He picked up the change and walked away.

There, now, wasn't that easy? The easiest, man, the very easiest. Now we find a phone booth.

A phone booth with particular advantages, though. A phone booth in a store that had two entrances, so he could slip in the back entrance without passing any cash registers or counters. Just slip in and hit the phone. Where was there a store like that? Lots of stores like that, but where exactly were they? It just took a little thinking, that's all. He thought. He walked as he thought.

Suppose he marched in through the back entrance and all the booths were occupied. That would be dandy, all right. He'd stand around with his red sleeve, and as soon as somebody spotted the sleeve, good-by, Johnny Lane.

Well, that was a chance he'd have to take. He found a cigar store on the third corner he passed. There was an entrance on the avenue and another on the side street. He glanced at the circular blue and white Bell telephone plaque set in the base of the store. Well, there was a telephone inside, at any rate. He turned the corner and walked to the glass-paned doorway. He stopped outside the doorway, trying to see the phone booths. He could see the booths, but only their sides, and he couldn't tell if they were empty or not. The back of the store was empty, though, so he'd have to make his play now if he was going to make it at all. Quickly he opened the door.

A bell over the door sounded, and he cursed these goddamn distrustful shopkeepers who put bells over every damn door. He shut the door quickly behind him, feeling the warmth of the shop, almost sighing heavily when he felt the warmth. He walked quickly to the phone booths, praying they were empty.

A thin man who looked like a bookie was in the first booth. He did not look up as Johnny passed him. He kept his mouth close to the mouthpiece, and he talked excitedly.

A woman was in the second booth. From the stupid grin on her face, she was talking to a man.

There was one more booth. He walked to it rapidly, the fingers on his left hand crossed.

The booth was empty. He stepped into it without looking behind him, closed the door, lifted the receiver from the hook, and deposited the dime quickly. He was not used to dialing Cindy's number with his left hand. He kept the receiver in his lap while he dialed, and then he put it to his ear hastily as the phone on the other end began ringing.

Come on, Cindy, he thought. Come on, baby, pick it up.

He counted the rings. He wondered what she was doing. He could almost see her phone where it rested on the stand in her apartment. He could see it as clearly as if he were there. He could almost see the instrument vibrating as it rang. And where was Cindy? On the other side of the room, at the stove or the icebox? She was walking across the apartment now, passing the bed, closer to the night table, reaching for it now, now her voice would come on the line.

The phone kept ringing. He fidgeted nervously in the booth.

Come on, baby, come on, he pleaded. Pick the goddamn thing up.

Was she taking a bath or something? Was that why she hadn't answered yet? He kept counting the rings. He let the phone ring twenty-two times, and then he hung up. He was not so much annoyed as he was puzzled. Why the hell hadn't she . . .

Time.

Time was back with him again. What time was it? He opened the door of the booth and stuck his head out, looking toward the front of the shop. An electric clock hung over the doorway, and he watched the sweep hand, and then focused his eyes on the hour and minute hands.

Nine-thirty-seven.

Well, sure. Well, no wonder. She was at the club already. She was probably getting ready for the first show now. He thought of her doing her dance, and then he had to force the thought out of his mind. She was at the club. If you're at the club, you can't answer the phone in your apartment.

Well, that let Cindy out. For the time being, anyway. But he still needed a coat, and he was hungry as hell. Just thinking of the coat made him feel cold again, and he wanted to stay in the warmth of the telephone booth forever. No, he couldn't do that. He had to get out of there soon, and that meant bucking the winds outside again. It wouldn't be so bad if he could put down a hot cup of java, but how could he walk into a restaurant with his arm looking the way it did?

He didn't want to chance going back to his own place. The cops would surely be watching there, and besides, he didn't want to get Molly in hot water. He began running through the list of people he knew, and the third person he came up with was Barney Knowles.

Sure, why not Barney? He knew Barney well. Barney would do him a few favors, especially with all the luck Barney'd been having lately. Sure, Barney would help a guy. Barney had a heart as big as Central Park.

He smiled.

He smiled, and then he left the phone booth and the store, and it was just as cold outside as it had been before.

There's a stretch of Harlem known as Striver's Row. It runs between Seventh and Eighth Avenues on West 138th and 139th Streets. It is not to be confused with the stretch east of Seventh Avenue on those same streets.

The streets in Striver's Row are tree-shaded. The houses lining those streets are made of attractive tan brick. The rents in Striver's Row are high, and most of the residents belong to the white-collar or professional class. Barney Knowles lived in Striver's Row.

He had not always lived in Striver's Row, mainly because he could not always afford the rental there. As a matter of fact, a good many of the people who'd been living there for a good long time rented out furnished rooms in order to keep up the rental. This was not one of Barney Knowles's problems. Barney never had any trouble keeping up the rental now. Not any more, he didn't.

Of course, it's doubtful that Barney's neighbors would have approved of him so readily if they'd known he was a bookie in the numbers racket. They saw only a rather portly, dark Negro who dressed conservatively, and who always had a cheerful smile for everyone he passed. The smile seemed doubly cheerful because there were two gold caps in the front of Barney's mouth, and you could usually see him coming two blocks away, even on a foggy day.

Barney liked Striver's Row. He liked it a lot, but he still kept his eye peeled for the day he could move to Sugar Hill.

A man's home is his castle, and Barney Knowles's home was just that to him. When he walked the streets of Striver's Row, the neighbors saw what he wanted them to see: the genial businessman, the smiling gent with the two gold teeth. When he closed the door of his apartment, he did as he wished.

On the night that Johnny Lane headed for Barney's pad, Barney was doing as he wished. His desire, on that night, was poker. His desire on almost every night, in fact, was poker. Barney was very lucky at cards, since the time his two front teeth had been knocked out. The teeth had been knocked out in a blackjack game when he was twenty-four. He had considered that the unluckiest night of his life, until

54

things began happening to him afterward. He later looked back to the loss of those teeth as the turning point in his career. At any rate, his later good fortune seemed to stem from the time he had the gold teeth put in. Barney nearly always won at cards now. To-night, Barney was losing.

He was not losing because his luck was running bad. Barney's luck never ran bad any more. He was losing because of the gentlemen in the game with him. The gentlemen owned the respective names of Arthur "The Flower" Carter and Anthony Bart. The gentlemen were very high up in the rackets indeed, and the gentlemen had an eye on Barney for a better job, and Barney had an eye on Sugar Hill, and so Barney lost that evening. Barney Knowles knew how to please.

He was laughing heartily at one of the jokes The Flower had told when the knock sounded on his door. He allowed himself the luxury of finishing his laugh, and then he said, "Excuse me, fellers, someone at the door."

The Flower, encouraged by the laughter that had greeted his last effort, asked, "You runnin' a whore house here, Barney?"

"Wisht I was," Barney answered, chuckling. He left the men in the living room and walked through the foyer to the front door. He kept the night latch on. A man in Barney's position never knew when a caller would be carrying a loaded gun. He unlocked the door and opened it to the extent the chain permitted.

He was not happy with what he saw standing in the hallway.

"Johnny," he said. "What are you doing here?"

"Everybody asks me the same question," Johnny said.

Barney looked over his shoulder toward the living room. The Flower was telling another joke, and Bart was listening respectfully. Bart never laughed. Bart only listened, and then maybe smiled if the joke was immensely funny.

"You'd better go, boy," Barney said. "This ain't the place for you."

"I'm cut, Barney. I'm cut bad. I ain't had anything to eat since—"

"Boy, your troubles don't interest me none. I got important people in here. If you led the cops to—"

"The cops are nowhere around," Johnny said. "I've been careful. Look, Barney—"

"Just a minute, boy," Barney said. He looked over his shoulder again, and then took the chain from its socket. He stepped out into the hallway and closed the door softly and rapidly behind him.

"What d'you mean, you're cut?" he asked.

"My arm," Johnny said. "I just stopped the bleeding."

Barney glanced at the bloodstained shirt. "You been to a doctor?"

"How can I go to a doctor? The cops are looking for me. You know that."

"Man, *do* I know it! You can ruin me by comin' here, Johnny. You shoulda had more sense than that."

"I need a coat, Barney, a jacket, anything. It's cold out there."

"Wait here," Barney said. "Don't move from that spot, and for God's sake, don't make any noise."

He opened the door quickly and stepped into the apartment again. He wiped the sweat from his forehead with a clean white handkerchief, and then he forced a smile onto his face. He was chuckling when he entered the living room.

"Who's that?" The Flower asked.

"Damn'est thing ever," Barney said, smiling. "Cleanin' boy. I promised to bring my overcoat in, an' I forgot all about it. Tailor thought I might need it, so he sent the boy up for it. Promised to have it back for me tomorrow."

"That's thoughtful," Bart said.

"Yeah, sure is. 'Scuse me a minute while I get it, will you?"

56

He walked out of the living room and into his bedroom. In the living room, Bart said, "You don't run 'cross thoughtful people much. Not in this racket."

"The tailor ain't in this racket," The Flower said, laughing.

Barney walked to his closet and opened the door. He had three overcoats, but he certainly wasn't going to give Johnny either of the two camel's-hair jobs. He took an old tweed coat from its hanger and started for the door again. He stopped short, considered for a moment, and then took a fiver from his wallet. He folded the bill and stuck it into the pocket of the coat. In the living room, The Flower was laughing at something else he'd just uttered. Bart was saying nothing.

Barney went into the living room. "You can deal the nex' hand, if you like," he said. "This won't take a minute."

"It's already dealt," The Flower said. "You got a king in the hole."

Barney laughed, and Bart said, "I don't get it."

The Flower began explaining why it was funny for him to know what Barney's hole card was, and Barney went to the door, opening it and stepping into the hallway again.

"Here's a coat," he whispered. "I stuck a fin into one of the pockets. Now get out of here, boy."

"Thanks, Barney. Thanks—"

"Skip it. Just scram. And listen, don't go gettin' any damn blood on that coat."

"I won't," Johnny promised. He slipped into the coat, feeling the bill in the left-hand pocket. "Thanks again, Barney."

Barney nodded and peered over his shoulder.

"Go on, boy," he whispered urgently.

Johnny started for the stair well. He was on the top step when Barney called, "Hey, boy."

Johnny turned. "Yeah?"

"You kill Luis?"

"No," Johnny said.

"I didn't figure. Go on, boy. Good luck."

Johnny smiled and ran down the steps. Barney waited until he was out of sight. He opened the door to his apartment then, and began chuckling automatically before he reached the living room.

Chapter Seven

The Club Yahoo was a small joint on Lenox Avenue. Its food was not particularly good, and its floor show— with the possible exception of Cindy Matthews—was just as bad. The prices on the liquor sold were rather high, and it's difficult to imagine why the club flourished. It *did* flourish, though, and perhaps that was due to the *danza exotica* Cindy performed there three times each night. It was a well-known fact that Sary Morgan, the owner and sole proprietor of the club, paid a good deal of change to the gendarmes for the privilege of allowing Cindy to perform her dance.

Sary—whose real name, Savannah, had been aborted to its present state years ago—was a rotund little man with a penchant for pretty girls. His floor show was studded with pretty if untalented, maidens, who formed an excellent backdrop for the dance Cindy performed. When the girls were not serving as a backdrop, they floated around among the customers, inducing them to drink. And whereas Sary had named the club "Yahoo" in all sincerity, there were those who insisted on calling it "Y'Whore."

It took a lot of deliberation for Johnny Lane to go there, and he went with some misgivings. But he wanted a place to spend the night, and he had to see Cindy about that. He didn't relish the idea of sleeping in some hallway. All he needed was some dame spotting him and screaming for the cops, figuring him for a drunk or something. No, he needed a place for the night, and Cindy was the only person he could think of now.

The Club Yahoo's bar started just inside the doorway, as if it were planned for someone to catch a quick shot with one foot outside the place. The bar ran the length of the right-hand wall in the long rectangular room. At the far end of the room a small platform sported a four-piece bop combo, and the combo was having at it hot and strong when Johnny entered the club. The tables lining the left-hand wall and then running perpendicular to the bar, leaving a square between the bandstand and the door for the floor show, were filled. The room was full of smoke and muted voices, and the bop combo blasted through the smoke with the precision skill of riveters.

A very dark trumpeter had his horn pointed at the draperies that hung from the ceiling of the joint. And even though the bell of his horn wore a straight mute, the draperies shook a little when he cut loose. The tenor-sax man kept up a slow, rocking harmony behind the trumpet, and the drums and piano socked out a rhythm while the horn shrieked. The boys seemed to gather momentum in the final chorus. The people at the tables began banging their glasses and clapping their hands in time with the beat. Johnny stood to the left of the entrance, and he felt his own foot tapping out the rhythm as the music spread to his body.

And then the tune ended abruptly, and the piano man threw his right hand at the keyboard, pulled out a sprinkling patter of notes and then stabbed them with some wild chords down in the bass. The drummer switched to brushes, keeping a rapid beat on the bass with one foot, lacing it with some high-hat work on the other foot. It was soft and quiet stuff, but quiet the way a .45 can be quiet when it's just sitting there and not shooting. There was a surging power behind the music, an eerie cacophony that wasn't quite cacophony, a dissonance that never became quite that. You expected a clinker, and then those black fingers spread over the white keys, and the clinker wasn't that at all; it became part of the melody again, a skillful twisting and intertwining of chords until the melody was almost obscured but never allowed to be completely smothered. It was good stuff, stuff with too much class for a dump like the Club Yahoo. The tenor and trumpet came in together, two B-flat horns blowing smoothly together, soft this time, but with that quiet roll of rhythm behind them. They scattered chords like gold pieces raining from the ceiling. They rode that melody like a chariot, and Johnny listened and lost himself in the music, lost himself in the swirling smoke and hushed voices, the clink of glasses at the bar, the dim lighting. With a band like that, a man had no need for a mootah high. The band gave you all the high you needed, and he listened and the music swelled inside him.

He felt the hand on his arm, and he turned his head abruptly.

The girl standing next to him was a light tan color, and she was wearing almost nothing but her color. Sary had decked her out in long black net stockings and a skirt that barely covered her. The skirt was part of a one-piece affair that hung loosely over her breasts, advertising the obvious fact that she wore no bra beneath it. Sary, a man who catered to fetishes, had given the girl garters to hold up the stockings, and the garters bit into her flesh tightly. She smiled brightly and leaned forward a little, the top of her garment falling away.

"Check your coat, sir?" she said.

"No, he answered. "No, thanks."

The girl kept her smile, but it lacked conviction now. The boys on the bandstand played a cute four bars that told the crowd they were taking a break, and Johnny huddled back against the wall, keeping away from the slightly brighter light of the check room. He didn't see Cindy anywhere around, but it was about time for her second show, and he figured it was safer waiting out here than going back to her. He'd try to catch her eye when she came on, and meanwhile he'd make himself as inconspicuous as possible.

He was trying to do just that when he spotted Hank Sands.

Sands was sitting at the bar, and he swung around on his stool and eyeballed the joint, his gaze passing the check room and then lingering on Johnny for an instant. Johnny wasn't sure he'd been seen. He started to turn his back, but he saw the smile come onto Sands' narrow mouth, and he cursed silently and waited.

Sands picked up his drink and sidled off the stool. The waiters were already hitting the tables, peddling their liquor during the band intermission. Sands worked his way through the activity, inching his way forward like a mole. He was a small man with a perpetual smirk on his mouth. He combed his hair in a high pompadour, aided by the various hair-straighteners he used. He also wore elevator shoes, but all his combined trickery didn't help his height any. He still looked like some kind of rodent, and the pegged pants and long jacket didn't help to conceal the slope of his shoulders or the narrowness of his chest or the mincing steps he took.

He was the kind of guy who made you feel slimy. There were a few guys like that in Johnny's immediate circle of acquaintances. Guys who could just stand there and say nothing and somehow make you feel as if spiders were crawling up your behind. Maybe it was the smirk Sands wore, like an open switch-blade knife. Or maybe it was his piggy little eyes. Or maybe it was the way he undressed every girl who came within three feet of him, sucking out her navel with his eyes. He'd visually undressed Cindy more times than Johnny could remember, and Sands certainly didn't try to hide the fact that he was intensely warm for her form. Cindy always looked uncomfortable when he ran over at the mouth. Johnny looked more than uncomfortable. Johnny had once almost ripped off Sands' head, but Sands had just laughed that infuriating high laugh of his and tried to pass it off as a joke.

The smirk was plastered on his mouth now as he worked his way over to Johnny. Johnny unconsciously glanced over his shoulder. He didn't trust Sands, and if the bastard was going to start yelling for the cops, he wanted to know where the door was and how quickly he could reach it.

Sands stopped in front of Johnny and examined him closely, the smile on his face.

"Well," he said, "dig the fugitive."

"Cool, man," Johnny warned.

"Ain' no cops here," Sands said. He stepped back a pace and studied Johnny again. "You doan look no different," he said.

"I don't feel no different," Johnny said. "What's on your mind, Sands?"

"I jus' wanted to know what a murd'rer looked like, thass all."

"I ain't killed nobody, Sands," Johnny said tightly.

"Ain't you, now? Well, now, thass a matter of 'pinion, now ain' it?"

Johnny said nothing. He hated the way Sands talked. Sands had been born and raised in Harlem, but he always tried to sound like a goddamn Georgia cotton-picker.

Sands was still smiling, enjoying Johnny's discomfiture immensely. "You reckon they goan send you to jail, man?"

"Not if I can help it," Johnny said.

"Murder." Sands shook his head. "Tch, tch, thass a shame. I understan' people gets cooked for murder. That right, Johnny? Does they fry people for murder?"

"Man, you're talking too much," Johnny said.

Sands chuckled shrilly. "Man," he said, "you kill me. I never done seen you so jumpy. You like a stick of tea, man? Sutthin' to calm you down?"

"I don't want nothing from you, Sands."

"On'y one thing I want fum you, Johnny," Sands said. "An' you know whut that is. An I sure's hell goan get it when they fry you."

"Look, you simple bastard . . ."

"Ah, ah, now le's watch that language, Johnny-boy. Le's jus' watch it now. Remember I jus' might get o-fended, and then I liable to wander over the phone

63

booths and call the bulls. Now, you doan want no bulls on the scene, does you?"

"Be the last phone call you ever made," Johnny said.

Sands chuckled again. "Yessir, boy. When they pop you in that chair and shaves off yo' hair, I'm goan come right down here and grab Cindy, right 'tween these two hands o' mine." He held his hands in front of him and tightened them, enjoying Johnny's helplessness. "Whutchoo think of that, man? Right 'tween these ol' fingers."

"Blow, Sands," Johnny said.

"I liable'a blow right over to the phone booths."

"Go ahead. You ever get strangled in a phone booth, you bastard?"

Sands smiled. He put his arm on Johnny's shoulder and said, "Man, I jus' teasin', thass all. No need to—"

"Take your hands off me! Blow!"

The smile dropped from Sands' mouth. His lips tightened, and he flicked angrily at his nose. He seemed about to say something further when the band began a slow melody, startling Johnny, because he hadn't known the musicians were back on the stand already. The lights in the club dimmed, and Sands started to move away from Johnny. Johnny reached out suddenly and caught him by the elbow.

"Stick around, Sands."

"Man, you jus' tole me to—"

"Stick around. I can't see the phone booths in the dark."

Sands chuckled again as a dim blue light suffused the small floor. A line of girls snaked its way from behind the bandstand. The girls wore wispy bras and G strings, and the blue light caught their sequined costumes and blinked across the club glitteringly. The girls carried small black hatboxes in their hands. They held the hatboxes aloft as they moved across the floor, lifting them over their heads as if they were making an offering to some deity up there someplace. The girls had been chosen by Sary for their busts and their legs. In the darkness, Johnny saw Sands wet his lips.

The girls wiggled their hips and then formed a semi-circle across the club, hiding the bandstand. The music stopped dead, and an amber spot scurried across the floor and then tacked itself to the curtain on the left of the bandstand.

Cindy Matthews was standing in that amber spot.

Cindy Matthews was fully clothed, but when the spot hit her, the club went suddenly silent. She leaned against the curtain like a panther ready to pounce. She was light-skinned, lighter than Johnny, with high cheekbones and the full flaring nostrils of a Negress. Her mouth was wide and sensuous, slashed now with lipstick. She wore her hair close to her head, giving an incongruous sophistication to the almost animal look of her face. She wore a flowing black gown that molded every line of her body. The gown's cape reached to her throat, billowing out where her breasts interrupted the straight tight line of the silk. Her ankles showed beneath the hem of the gown, and her feet were in black high-heeled pumps, sequined to catch the beam of the amber spot.

She wore long black gloves, reaching to the elbow, and she put both hands on her hips now and came onto the floor, standing in front of the almost nude chorus as the musicians waited. She smiled a dazzling smile and then began taking off the gloves. At the same instant, the girls behind her got to their knees. They put the hatboxes on the floor and took off the lids, moving together—or almost together—while Cindy peeled off the gloves. And as she peeled, the chorus removed gloves from the hatboxes and began pulling them on, working in reverse, so that when Cindy dropped her second glove to her feet, the girls in the chorus were wearing gloves on both hands.

"She gasses me," Hank Sands whispered. "Man, she really—"

"Shut up," Johnny whispered back.

The music had started again. It was not a tortuous kind of music, and there was no suggestion of sensuality in it. Cindy's dance was not that kind of dance.

If it had been that kind of dance, that obviously titillating bump-and-grind thing, the cops might have been willing to ignore it, and Sary Morgan might have saved the monthly payoff. But it was not that. She performed no acrobatics with the curtain. After the one warm smile she flashed at her audience, she smiled no more. She was totally unaware of the audience, the music, and the chorus behind her.

It was almost as if a crowd of people had gathered behind a screen in her bedroom. Cindy Matthews had come home from a ball, and Cindy Matthews was now undressing for bed. And while she undressed, the girls behind her dressed, but no one was watching the girls behind her. Every eye in the joint was on Cindy Matthews. There was no catcalling and no whistling. There was a respectful silence, because all these people were in Cindy's own bedroom, behind that screen in the corner, and they didn't want to make any noise lest she find out they were there.

Cindy was just a woman taking off her clothes.

She was nothing more and nothing less. She was exciting only in the way a beautiful woman can be exciting performing this simplest of tasks.

And that's why Sary paid off the cops. Once you saw Cindy Matthews undress, you could stuff all the bumps and grinds into an old top hat and dump it in the Harlem River.

There was no coyness in her routine. There was no attempt to tease. There was only a sinuous gracefulness, an intimacy that made every man in the place feel she was undressing for him alone, an intimacy that made every female spectator feel vastly inadequate.

She started with the gloves, and then she removed the cape at the top of her dress, revealing rounded shoulders and a low-cut gown with a deep, soft hollow between her breasts. She kept on her shoes, but she began unbuttoning the side of the gown, one button at a time, revealing the curve of her calf, and then her knee, and then part of her thigh, and then she stopped unbuttoning and reached behind her for the zipper at the back of her dress.

She turned as she lowered the zipper, and the audience watched the tightness of the dress across her buttocks, and then their eyes fled to her hand on the zipper as it lowered slowly, the dress parting in a wide V over the smooth tan flesh of her back. The girls behind her stepped into their gowns, began pulling them up over ankle and calf and knee and thigh, hiding the sequined G strings.

Cindy lowered the zipper until it reached the base of her spine, until the tight band of the G string showed above her buttocks. The biting slender line of her brassiere cut into her back, and she whirled suddenly, catching the bodice of her gown before it fell. She looked up and toward the back of the club, and that was when she saw Johnny.

He knew she'd seen him. He saw the sudden flash in her eyes, and then the flash died and she went through the rest of her dance, but he knew she'd seen him.

She dropped the gown away from her breasts, showing the filmy, sequined bra that encased them. She crossed her arms over her waist, holding up the gown, embracing herself with her head thrown back, her breasts tilted and high. And then she brought her hands away from her body, and the gown slipped down over her wide hips, dropped below her navel, slithered past the sequined G string, fell to her feet in a black lifeless heap. She stood there for a moment, her gaze on the floor, a woman unaware, a woman full-breasted and long-legged, standing in high-heeled pumps, wearing only a bra and a G string, bathed in an amber light.

And then she reached behind her for the clasp of her bra, and the girls behind her, fully dressed now, threw their gloved hands upward as the brassiere fell from Cindy's firm breasts.

There was a sudden blackout, and when the lights came on again, the stage was as naked as Cindy had been. The applause burst from a hundred pairs of hands, shattering the stillness of the club. Johnny listened to the applause, and he felt a mixture of emotions: pride because the applause was for his Cindy; anger because the applause was cheering the lust she'd aroused.

"Mmmm-mmmm," Sands said. "Man, I like to get a piece of that."

"Sands, you slimy bastard, I'm going to—"

"Hesh now, man. You doan want to 'tract 'tention, do you?"

"Just keep your dirty mind off Cindy, that's all."

"Li'l hard to do that when she undressin' out there," Sands said, smiling. "Here she come now, boy, all dressed up. She a quick dresser, ain' she?" Sands paused. "She a even quicker *un*dresser, I bet."

He saw Cindy weaving her way through the club. She walked proudly, with her shoulders back, wearing a simple cocktail dress now. There was a serious look on her face, and her lips were held tightly together, but she walked with unhurried grace.

"Cut out," Johnny said to Sands.

"Want to say hello to Cindy," Sands said stubbornly, not moving.

She came to Johnny quickly, and her eyes searched his face.

"Are you all right?" she asked breathlessly.

"I got cut," he said. He remembered Sands abruptly. He turned to face him, and he saw Sands' eyes on the bodice of Cindy's dress, and he felt his fists clench.

"Hello, Cindy," Sands said.

"Hello, Hank," she said wearily.

"Mighty nice dance out there."

"Thank you."

"Like to make my blood boil."

"Get the hell out of here, Sands," Johnny said.

"Why, sure thing, man. Glad to o-blige." Sands laughed shrilly and squeezed past Cindy, his hand brushing her thigh lightly.

"That sonovabitch," Johnny said.

"Never mind him. You said you got cut. Is it all right now?"

"I stopped the bleeding. Honey, I need a place to stay. I thought . . ."

Cindy reached into the front of her gown. "Here's a key to my place. Go there, Johnny. It'll be all right. You'll be safe."

"The cops. What'd they—"

"Nothing. I told them we'd broke up."

"You shouldn't have said that, honey."

"It was the only thing to do, Johnny. This way, they won't bother me again, maybe. Johnny, I don't trust Hank. I think you'd better go before . . ."

"Honey, I didn't kill him. You know that, don't you?"

"It doesn't matter," Cindy said softly.

"I know it doesn't, but I wanted you to know anyway. I didn't kill Luis."

"All right," Cindy said. "That's good enough for me."

Johnny smiled. "I liked your dance too, Cindy."

"Go, Johnny. Please. The cops may walk in any minute."

"You'll be home later?"

"Yes, of course."

"I'll wait up for you."

"All right. Hurry, Johnny, please."

"Cindy?"

"Yes?"

"I love you."

"All right."

"No, I mean it. I love you."

"I know, Johnny." She glanced over her shoulder and then reached up suddenly, finding his mouth with her own. She kissed him fleetingly, hardly a kiss at all, only a brushing of lips.

"Hurry, darling. I'll see you later. There's food in the icebox." She smiled abruptly. "Take care of yourself. I love you."

She squeezed his hand and then walked to the bar,

and he watched her go. He felt the key in the palm of his hand, closed his fingers on it, and left the club quickly.

He caught a cab on the next corner, and the cab took him up Lenox and then over to Seventh Avenue and 142nd Street. He got out at the corner, paid and tipped the cabbie, and was starting up the street when he saw the white-topped squad car parked in front of Cindy's building.

The sight of the car was like a knife in the ribs. He viciously slammed his fist into the open palm of his other hand. The door of the squad car opened, and Johnny looked at it only once more and then turned and ran.

Chapter Eight

Detective First/Grade David Trachetti wondered just why the hell he was knocking himself out. He stepped out of the squad car and onto the asphalt, holding the door open.

"This'll only be a few minutes, Stan," he said.

"Take all the time you need," the uniformed cop behind the wheel said.

Trachetti nodded and slammed the door shut, then walked around the grille of the car to the sidewalk. He checked the address on his pad with the one over the door, and then he started up the steps to the stoop.

An old couple was sitting on the stoop, huddled against the cold. He wondered why anyone in his right mind would sit outside on a night like this, and he nodded briefly as he passed the couple. The couple did not nod back. They stared at him hostilely. He was white, and he was a cop, and that made him a double menace. Trachetti felt the coldness of their stares at the back of his neck, and he wondered again why the hell he was bothering. Did any of them appreciate it? Hell, he might very well get knifed, just the way Palazzo had said he would.

Well, to hell with Palazzo. There was such a thing as carrying it too far. What the hell, if the kid was out there thinking he was wanted for a kill, somebody should tell him he was cleared. The girl had told Palazzo that she and Lane had broken up, but that might have been a lie. Trachetti would tell her how they'd caught the killer, and then let her get the word to her boy friend. That was the sensible thing to do, wasn't it? All right, maybe it wasn't the sensible thing to do. Maybe he should have sat back at the precinct, where it was nice and warm. Maybe he should have sat on his behind there and listened to the tired jokes the boys were telling. Or there was still the Nunzio case, and the prints he'd given the lab boys, and he could have gone down there to see what they'd made on it. They hardly ever got a make from prints, though, so there wasn't much sense to that. And besides, it bothered him, this Johnny Lane thing.

He struck a match and glanced down the long row of mailboxes. As in most apartment buildings in Harlem, there were three and four surnames on each letter box. He found the box marked C. Matthews. Apartment 42. He shook out the match and climbed the stairs.

The numbers on the door must have been bright and new at one time. They were tarnished and bent now, and the 2 dangled from one screw.

He looked for a bell button, and when he found there was none, he used his knuckles on the door. He rapped lightly because it was late at night, and he didn't want to cause more disturbance than he had to. When he got no answer, he rapped again.

"Miss Matthews?" he called softly.

A door opened, but it wasn't the door he knocked on. A man in his undershirt came out into the hallway, two doors down from Cindy's.

"Whutcha want?" he asked.

"I'm looking for Miss Matthews," Trachetti said, "Cynthia Matthews. Would you know if she's home?"

"She ain't home," the man said. He continued to stare at Trachetti suspiciously.

"Do you know where she is?"

"No," the man lied.

"I'm not trying to harm her. I want—"

"I don't know where she is," the man said.

"You're sure she's not home?"

"She ain't home," the man said.

"Well. Thank you."

The man walked into his apartment and slammed the door behind him, and Trachetti listened to the slam

72

in the dim hallway, and he couldn't say he blamed the man very much. Still, he was trying to do the girl a favor. I mean, he thought, what the hell. I came here to help her.

Did she work nights? He wished he'd checked her card more carefully. He'd scanned it quickly for her address, before Palazzo could catch him at it and make some crack, and now he'd made a trip for nothing.

Oh, what the hell. What the hell is a man supposed to do, anyway?

He walked down the steps quickly and out onto the stoop. The old man and woman were still sitting there, breathing the cold November air. Trachetti saw the hostility in their eyes, and then he turned his head away and went to the squad car.

"I drew a blank," he said to the driver.

The driver shrugged and opened the door for Trachetti.

Johnny knocked on the closed door urgently, and when he realized there was a bell, he saved his knuckles and pressed his forefinger against the button. He could hear the sound of laughter inside the apartment, and then the sound of the bell knifing the laughter, cutting it off. He kept his finger on the button and inside he heard Barney Knowles shout, "All right, stop leanin' on the damn thing!"

He shouldn't have done that, he shouldn't have leaned on the bell. The one thing he didn't want to do was get Barney sore at him. With the cops at Cindy's place, he needed Barney again. Barney would know what to do.

He heard Barney's heavy footsteps inside, and then someone laughed again, and then the door snapped back, and the chain pulled taut, and he saw Barney's face, plastered with a smile that dropped suddenly, leaving a mouth open in a small O.

"Johnny, for God's sake—"

"I had to come back. Believe me, Barney, I wouldn't have if I—"

Barney was already shaking his head. His eyes said no even before his mouth did. "Kid, go away. Now look, I'm not kidding. The answer is no. Whatever you want, it's no."

"Barney, I ain't got a place to stay. I can't walk the streets. They'll pick me up, sure as hell."

"Well, you can't stay here, kid. Now look, let's be sensible about this. I mean, even if you—"

"Who is it, Barney?" The Flower called from the living room.

Barney hesitated. "Nobody, Flower."

"Must be *some*body," The Flower called back.

"Now you done it," Barney said. "*God*damnit, now you done it!"

"Hey, Barney!" The Flower yelled. "Who is it?"

"Look, kid," Barney said hastily, "I gave you a fin. Use it. Here, here's another five. Get a room someplace. That'll keep you off the streets. Kid, I can't do no more than that for you. Now, here, take this. Come on, kid."

"How can I get a room? Don't you think the cops are checking all the hotels and rooming joints? Barney, I wouldn't be here if I could've taken a room. I got dough, that ain't a problem."

"You need any help, Barney?" The Flower called, and Johnny heard the scrape of a chair, and then footsteps approaching the door.

"Oh, Lord," Barney muttered. He sighed heavily and then reached for the chain, pulling the door wide. "Come on in," he said wearily.

Johnny went into the apartment just as The Flower came from the living room. The Flower looked Johnny over and then asked, "Who's this, Barney?" At the same time his hand casually strayed to the lapel of his jacket, and Johnny saw the bulge of his shoulder holster under the cut of his suit.

"He's on the run," Barney said, deciding to play it straight.

"Oh?" The Flower's eyebrows rose in interest. "What you done, kid?"

"Nothing," Johnny answered. "They think I killed Luis the Spic, but I didn't."

There was the sound of another chair being shoved back in the living room, and then more footsteps. Anthony Bart poked his head around the corner.

"What's goin' on?" he asked.

"Kid here on the lam," The Flower said.

"Yeah?"

"They hangin' a frame on him."

"What kind of frame?" Bart asked.

"Murder," The Flower replied.

"What's he doin' here?" Bart asked Barney.

"He . . . he . . ."

"I ain't got a place to stay," Johnny said. "I thought Barney could help me. Barney knows a lot of people."

"This your cleanin' boy, Barney? That your coat he's wearin'?"

"Yes," Barney said softly.

"You ain't got a place to stay, huh, man?"

"No," Johnny said.

"You lead the bulls here?" The Flower asked.

"No."

"You sure?" Bart put in.

"I'm positive."

"Mmmm."

"So you the one killed that spic, huh?" The Flower said.

"No, I didn't kill him."

"You jus' now told me it was a frame," Bart said to The Flower.

"I know. I was figurin' we might have a spot for somebody handy with a gun."

"I didn't kill him," Johnny said.

"Yeah, I know that. That's what you said, ain't it?"

"That's what I said."

"Still . . ." The Flower paused. "What you think, Bart?"

"I don't know. What're you thinkin'?"

"Hate to see the cops get their mitts on anybody. I mean, *any*body. You know what I mean?"

"Keep out of it." Bart said. "It's his headache."

"Why, sure. no doubt about it. Still, I hate to see the cops happy. Don't you feel the same way?"

"I don't feel no way," Bart said. "I ain't yearnin' for an accessories after."

"Why, the boy just said he didn't do it!" The Flower said.

"They all say that." Bart answered. "Man, if I had a cent for every time I said *I* didn't do it!"

"I didn't." Johnny insisted.

"Yeah. I know. This guy just killed hisself."

"I'll get rid of him," Barney said. "You fellows go back to the game."

"No, wait a minute," The Flower said. "What you think, Bart?"

"I already told you what I think. This boy's hot. I don't want none of him to burn me."

"Look, Johnny." Barney said. "Why don't you go? Can't you see all the trouble you're causin'?"

"We don't have to touch it at all," The Flower said meditatively. "We call some of the boys, and they'll take care of it. We don't have to come nowheres near it."

"When there's a kill stinkin' up the joint," Bart said, "it ain't possible to come nowhere near it. Some of it rubs off. Let it lie, Flower. Get rid of the kid."

"No," The Flower said slowly. "I don't think so."

"Flower, I can handle this," Barney said. "Just let me—"

"Shut up, Barney!" The Flower said. "Where's your phone?"

"In the living room. You . . . you think we should help him, Flower?"

"We ain't gonna help nobody," the Flower said. "Jus' remember that. We never even seen this kid. We jus' gonna make a few phone calls, that's all." The Flower walked into the living room.

"He's a crazy bastard," Bart said. shaking his head. He looked at Johnny significantly. "Nex' time, tell your friends to stay away from here, Barney."

"Is it my fault he come?" Barney asked. "Hell, I give him a coat and a fin. Ain't that enough? Did I tell him to come back here?"

They walked into the living room as The Flower dialed and waited for his party. In a moment he said, "This is Flower. Who's around?"

He listened and then said, "I need two boys and a car. . . . What? . . . No, a short trip. . . . No, nothin' like that. Look, this is a routine job, now don't give me a third degree. . . . Well, all right. I need them right away. . . . What? . . . Right away means right away, what the hell you think it means? . . . Right away, five minutes . . . Yeah, just a minute."

He covered the mouthpiece with one hand and asked Barney, "What's your address, man?"

"They're going to come *here*?"

"Where you think they going—Grant's tomb?"

"I just thought it might be better—"

"What's your address?"

Barney gave him the address, and The Flower repeated it into the phone.

"You got that now? . . . Have them come up and ring the bell. . . . What? . . . Oh, just a secon'."

He covered the mouthpiece again. "What's your apartment number?"

"Three-C," Barney said.

"Three-C," The Flower said to the mouthpiece. "I'll 'spec you in five minutes. . . . Yeah, yeah, all right. . . . Yeah, that's fine. Just get them here, that's all."

He hung up abruptly. "They'll be here in five minutes," he said.

"Thanks," Johnny said.

"You want to play a few rounds while we wait?" The Flower asked. "Watched pot never boils, you know." He waited for his laugh, and when he got none, he provided it himself.

The boys arrived in seven minutes flat. One stayed at the wheel of the black Buick downstairs. The other

77

rang the doorbell and stepped into the apartment as soon as the door was open. The Flower told him where to go, and the big man just nodded and then led Johnny out of the apartment.

Neither of the two men spoke during the ride.

When Johnny asked, "Where we going?" they both shrugged. He sat between them uneasily, wondering whether or not The Flower's idea of helping was the same as his own. He began to recognize landmarks then, and he said, "Hey, we going to the river?"

The driver nodded.

"I don't get it," Johnny said.

"A boat," the driver said, and that was all he said until they reached the Harlem River. They doused the lights on the car and then worked their way over the discarded oil drums and assorted garbage leading down to the riverbank. There was hardly any moon, and Johnny didn't see the boat until they were almost upon it.

"That it?" he asked.

"Mmm," one of the men said.

"Won't the cops look here?"

"This boat's been here for years. Hole in the back end," one of the men said. "You sleep up front, and you won't get wet. Don't worry about cops, they won't look for you here."

"I don't know," Johnny said dubiously.

The driver laughed. "Only thing you got to worry about here is rats."

"Rats!"

"Size of your head." The driver laughed again. "You get down there, boy. We got to cut out."

They helped Johnny into the gutted boat, and he watched them climb back up to the car. He stood in the bow until the car pulled away. They did not turn on their lights until they were several blocks in the distance.

The boat was not a large one. Its bow was pulled up onto the bank, and Johnny could hear the water lapping against the stern plankings, inside the boat. A cold moistness blew off the river, and he bundled his coat around his throat and tried not to smell the aroma of garbage. There was a small cabin up forward, and he went into it and tried to make himself comfortable on the deck. The windows of the cabin were shattered. The entire boat, in fact, looked as if it might slip into the water at any moment, giving up the struggle with the elements. Well, at least it was safe from the cops, and a place to spend the night.

If only the cops hadn't been watching Cindy's place. Damnit, why were all the breaks running against him? A rat like Luis gets . . . Rats, they said.

Only thing you got to worry about here is rats.

He didn't like rodents. He hadn't liked them since he was seven years old, shortly after his mother had died. There used to be a big vase on the mantel, and Molly used to drop nickels and dimes into it. He'd wanted an ice-cream pop one night, and Molly wasn't home, so he'd pulled a chair over to the mantel and reached into the vase for a nickel. He'd felt sharp teeth clamp onto his middle finger, and he'd screamed and yanked his hand out of the vase. A mouse was clinging to his finger. It was a tiny little thing, gray, and it loosened its grip almost instantly, falling to the floor and scurrying away for its hole.

But terror had struck deep within Johnny when he'd felt that mouse's teeth and seen its furry shape. The terror had remained with him. He could not even *think* of mice or rats without feeling a shudder of apprehension.

Thinking of them now, he felt a cold chill start at the base of his spine travel up his back until he brought the wings of his shoulders together in an involuntary tremor.

He sat with his back against the cabin of the boat, and he listened to the lapping of the water in the stern, and the creaking of the wood, and the city noises in the distance. He started at every sound, and his eyes pierced the darkness, wary, afraid.

He thought he heard a rat once, and he leaped to his feet, only to discover it was a loose piece of canvas flapping against the cabin top.

He did not sleep that night.

Chapter Nine

It was morning in Harlem, morning on the day after Luis Ortega was shot to death with a zip gun. A foggy mist clung to the roofs of the tenements, spread its gray tentacles over concrete and brick, swirled around the television antennas and the back-yard clotheslines.

For Johnny there was a vast nothingness of gray fog that smothered the boat and the river and the riverbank, that smothered everything the day held for him. Somewhere in that gray fog was the man who'd killed Luis Ortega, and somewhere out there were the cops, too, but the cops were looking for Johnny and not the man who'd really done the job. He'd sat awake all night, and his body was stiff now, and he could barely keep his eyes open. He did not want to leave the boat, and yet he sensed the boat would not be safe during the daylight hours. He had to leave the boat, but he felt too weary to make it to the street, and he wondered if he would simply collapse, making the job nice and easy for the cops.

He was hungry again, too, and his arm was beginning to pain him, a dull sort of pain that gnawed at his elbow. He needed help, and he couldn't go to Barney Knowles again, not after the trouble he'd caused last night, but neither could he walk the streets, because he would most certainly collapse.

He didn't want to go to his own place because the cops would be there sure as hell, and he didn't want Molly to get in trouble. You shouldn't go around getting your own sister in trouble, not when she was the one who raised you.

There must be a lot of places I can go, he thought. I'm not the first guy who was ever hunted, and I won't be the last guy. They hole up somewhere, I know that, but where? There are a lot of places, and I *know* there are a lot of places, but I can't think of any offhand. If I *had* murdered Luis, I'd have picked out a spot to hide beforehand, but I didn't murder Luis, and so I didn't think that far ahead.

Someone murdered Luis, and I should be out looking for him, but how can I look for him when everybody else is looking for me?

Now we're thinking clearly, he told himself. Now we have the world where the hair is short. All I have to do is find the killer before the police find me. That's simple.

Except I'm tired, I'm so goddamn tired. Why'd they have to tell me about the rats? Why couldn't they have kept their fat mouths shut? I'd have slept if I hadn't known. Sure, and then I'd have had my throat ripped out in my sleep.

The thought chilled him. He shuddered, and then climbed wearily out of the boat and began climbing the embankment.

I've got to try Cindy again, he thought. Maybe the cops got tired and went home. Besides, what is she thinking by now? Hell, she gave me a key and I never used it. She probably thinks I'm lying dead in some gutter. I've got to get to Cindy's.

He was glad to be doing something again, glad to have set a goal for himself. As he walked, he felt the stiffness leave his body, but the fuzziness was still inside his head, and he knew he had to get some sleep soon. He could get sleep at Cindy's. He could sleep curled up in her arms.

He thought of Cindy, and he walked steadily toward her apartment, keeping the collar of his coat turned up against the fog. He was glad for the fog now. The fog hid him, and he wanted to be hidden. If only his arm didn't hurt so much, and if only he weren't so sleepy, if only he'd had a little more to eat, if ony he knew who'd killed Luis.

When he reached her street, he looked down it quickly. There was no squad car in sight. That didn't mean anything, of course. The cops might be hiding out in a building across the street, just waiting for him to show. Well, he'd have to chance that. If they wanted him that bad, if they wanted him bad enough to stop him from getting the sleep he needed, well, they could have him. He was getting tired of all this running, anyway. How long can you run without getting tired?

He walked down the street, his head low, his hands in his pockets. When he reached her building, he did not turn to look over his shoulder. He went up onto the stoop and then into the hallway, and then up the steps to the fourth floor without once looking behind him.

He walked directly to Apartment 42, fished the key out of his pocket, and was inserting it into the lock when Cindy's voice came from behind the door, startled.

"Who is it?"

"It's me," he whispered. "Johnny."

He heard the rustle of bedclothes behind the door, and he twisted the key and pushed the door open, stepping inside and locking it quickly behind him. He saw her long legs as she stepped out of bed, and then she was running toward him, wearing a pajama top buttoned to the throat, looking very much like a little girl except for the firm outlines of her breasts beneath the pajama top, and the long curves of her legs.

She threw herself into his arms, and he held her close, leaning against the door, feeling the warmth of her against him.

"Johnny, Johnny, I was so worried!"

"It's all right," he said, soothing her, his palms open flat against her back. He could feel the smoothness of her skin beneath the pajama top. She sucked in a deep breath that caught in her throat, and he felt the tremor that passed through her body. She pulled away from him suddenly, holding him at arm's length, looking up into his face. She wore no make-up, and the light passing through the drawn window shade put a pale yellow tint onto her face. Her eyes were clear, and she parted her lips slightly as she studied his face.

"Are you all right?"

"I'm sleepy," he said.

"Your arm. Is it all right?"

"It's all right. It hurts, but it's not bleeding any more."

"I'll give you a bandage."

"It has a bandage."

"A fresh one," she said. Her voice was edged with sleep, and they both whispered unconsciously, he too tired to use a full voice, and she talking with the muted voice of someone who'd just come from a warm bed. "Take off your coat, darling."

He took off the coat, wincing when it slid off his right arm.

"Does it hurt bad?"

"Yes. Yes, it does. Well, not too bad."

"Come on. Lie down."

She led him to the bed, and he flopped onto it, feeling the warm sheet beneath him, and under that the softness of the mattress.

"This is good," he said, sighing.

"What happened last night?" she asked. She walked to the bathroom, and he watched the loose pajama top flap idly above her legs, just covering the curve of her buttocks.

"Cops here," he said. "Downstairs."

"Here?" she asked, rummaging through the medicine chest.

"Mmm. Downstairs."

"They weren't here when I came home. Johnny, I was worried to death. I didn't know what to think."

"I stayed in a boat on the river. Some of Barney's friends took me there."

"Barney Knowles?"

"Yes."

She came back into the room with a roll of gauze and

84

a bottle of iodine. She put down her medicine and bandage, and then fluffed up the pillows behind him. Quickly she began unbuttoning his shirt. When she pulled the sleeve from his right arm, he opened his mouth in pain.

"I'm sorry, darling," she said.

"It just hurt for a minute. The cloth was stuck."

She unwrapped the bandage from his arm, and when she saw the cut she blanched.

"Johnny, I . . . I think we should get a doctor."

"No," he said.

"Your arm . . ."

"No doctor. Honey, we can't take the chance."

She bit her lip and nodded, and then she opened the bottle of iodine and poured a little of it into the cut.

An "Agh-agh-agh-agh" sound rushed from Johnny's open mouth as the iodine began to sting. Cindy poured it into the cut more freely now, and then she began bandaging the arm again. He felt the gauze tighten there, and he began to feel a little better. The pillows were very soft, very, very soft.

"I want to sleep in your arms," he said.

"All right," she answered.

"Do you mind?"

"No," she said softly.

"I know it's crazy, but that's what I want. Can you understand, Cindy?"

"I understand."

"Cindy, why do you work in that club? Cindy, I wish you wouldn't, I mean it."

"Yes, darling," she said.

His eyes were beginning to close, and he fought to keep them open. She pulled off his trousers, and then pulled the blanket to his neck.

"Cindy, really, I wish you wouldn't work at the club."

"We'll see, darling," she said.

She climbed in beside him and said, "Lift your head a little, darling."

He lifted his head and her arm slid beneath his neck. With her other hand she tilted his head down until it rested in the hollow of her shoulder, her sloping breast soft against his cheek.

"Now sleep," she said. "Sleep, Johnny. Everything's going to be all right."

"Suppose the cops—"

"Never mind the cops. Just sleep, baby." She began stroking his hair with her fingers, and he felt the length of her body against his, warm, supple.

He tilted his head up and kissed her on the mouth. She kissed him with her eyes open, looking at his face as it came closer to hers.

Then his head was on her breast again, and she heard his heavy breathing become slow and even, and she knew he was asleep. She kissed him on the forehead and held him close.

"Looks like the sun's trying to come out," the patrolman said.

"Yes. Yes, it does."

The patrolman had time to kill. He didn't have to call in yet, and there'd been no activity this morning. Probably half of Harlem was still in bed.

"There's nothing like a dreary day in Harlem," he expanded. "Why is it that nothing can get as dreary as a dreary day in Harlem?"

"Well, I don't know."

"That's the trouble with you people," the patrolman said, "you don't know nothing."

He pulled a sour face and leaned against the counter.

"If I lived in Harlem, you can bet your ass I'd know all about it. Why, I'll bet right now, not even living here, just working here, I know more about Harlem than three-fourths of the Nigras in it."

"That may be so."

"Damn tootin' it's so. I can give you the location of every whore house and every drop. I know where all the shooting galleries are, and I can give you the names

86

of everybody in Harlem pushing dope." The patrolman nodded his head solemnly.

"If you know all this, why don't the police clean it up?"

"I can see you don't know nothing about the way we operate."

"Well, to tell the truth, I don't."

"The point is to keep it all out in the open," the patrolman said. "This way we know where it all is, and we can crack down whenever we like. If we raided one whore house now, all the rest would go underground. Then where would we be?"

"Well, what's the difference? I mean, if you know where they are and don't crack down, they might just as well be underground."

"You just don't understand," the patrolman said. "This is politics."

"Oh, I see."

"Now, don't go getting ideas. I don't mean graft. I mean we work a kind of politics in Harlem, you understand?"

"A little."

"What's the sense talking to you? You just don't understand." The patrolman wiped a beefy hand over his face and then looked through the plate-glass window. "Yep, the sun *is* coming out. Happy day."

"It *was* pretty gray."

"Pretty gray is putting it mild. You could cut that fog with a razor." The patrolman paused. "You carry a razor?"

"Me?"

"Yes, you."

"That's a funny question to ask. Why should I carry a razor?"

"How should I know? Why does every other Nigra in Harlem carry a razor?"

"Well, I don't know if that's true or not."

"That's what I mean," the patrolman said. "You live right here, and you don't know what the hell's going on right under your nose. Every Nigra carries a razor."

"I don't."

"Then you're the exception that proves the rule," the patrolman said righteously.

"You've got a pretty stereotyped picture of the Negro, I'd say."

"A pretty *what* picture?"

"Never mind."

The patrolman toyed with some of the items on the counter. "You mean you think the folks in Harlem *don't* carry razors, is that it?"

"Some do, I imagine. But just as many don't."

"They're crazy if they don't," the patrolman said. "You never know when you're gonna get killed in Harlem. Knifed or razored or zip-gunned or what the hell. You should know that, you live here."

"I've never had any trouble."

"That's what they all say until they feel that knife in their ribs." The patrolman nodded sourly. "Look what happened to that sonovabitch Ortega. There's one guy who thought he was riding high. So what happens? Bam, with a zip gun. He ain't riding high no more, he sure ain't."

"Luis wasn't exactly what I'd call an average citizen."

"There ain't no average citizen. What the hell are you doing, selling statistics? Luis the Spic was like everybody else in Harlem, no more, no less."

"I don't think—"

"He," the patrolman said, raising his voice, "thought he knew all the angles. Only angle he didn't figure was the trajectory of a bullet, and that's a curve." The patrolman laughed suddenly. "Well, serves the bastard right. I'm almost sorry they got the guy who done it."

"They . . . they caught him?"

"Sure. Few hours after it happened. You can't put nothing over on the cops in Harlem, feller, just remember that."

"I didn't know. I mean, I didn't know they caught him."

The patrolman beamed proudly, as if he'd been the one who'd made the arrest. "We got him, all right," he said.

"That's a shame. I mean, about Johnny Lane. He was a nice kid. We sort of gr—"

"Johnny Lane? No, no, he's not the one."

"But you said—"

"You talking about the guy who had the fight with Luis a while back? Yeah, we thought it was him, too. But it's another guy who done it. Brown, Charlie Brown. You ever hear of him?"

"No. No, I . . . You mean Johnny didn't kill Luis?"

"This Brown guy plugged him. He shot him 'cause Luis wouldn't fix him. Bam, all over for the spic." The patrolman inflated his chest. "We got him, though." He began chuckling suddenly. "Hey, you want to hear something funny?"

"What?"

"This other guy, this Lane character. He don't even know we got the killer yet." The patrolman burst out laughing. "He thinks the law is still after him! Ain't that something?"

"He doesn't know? But . . . but shouldn't—"

"He'll find out sooner or later," the patrolman said, his laugh subsiding.

"But how? Who'll tell him?"

"Hell, *you* can tell him, if you feel like it."

"Me?"

"Sure, go ahead. Do it with our blessings." The patrolman scratched his jaw. "Well, I better call in. Looks like it's gonna be a nice day, after all."

"Yes."

"So long, feller. Keep things running right, huh?"

"Yes, I will. Yes, thank you."

The patrolman walked through the store and then pulled open the door. The bell over the door sounded when he opened it. He waved back at the counter, and then walked out onto the sidewalk.

There was now one man in Harlem—with the exception of the police—who knew that Johnny Lane had been cleared.

That man leaned on the counter in Lefkowitz's drugstore and bit his lip worriedly.

That man was Frankie Parker.

Chapter Ten

This was definitely a curious turn of events, Frankie thought.

Was it possible that Johnny really hadn't killed the spic? Well, that's what the patrolman had said. It seemed unlikely, but the police didn't make mistakes like that, not when it concerned murder. Charlie Brown? Did he know anyone named Charlie Brown? None that he could think of. There was an old man who came into the store every now and then, but his name was Bernard Brown, so he wasn't the one.

Charlie Brown, Charlie Brown . . . Well, it wasn't really important.

The important thing, of course, was the fact that Johnny was innocent. And, according to what the cop had said, Johnny didn't even know he'd been cleared. Frankie shook his head in wonder.

He had certainly seemed guilty yesterday. Was it only yesterday? Yes, and he'd looked damned guilty. That harried look on his face, and the bleeding arm. Of course, there's something about blood that immediately indicates violence. How was Frankie, after all, to know that he was innocent? Was he supposed to take a chance helping Johnny when he *might* have been guilty, when he certainly looked guilty? Everybody was saying he'd killed the spic, and then he showed up with the ripped arm, so who was a person supposed to believe? Everybody, or Johnny?

I did dress his arm, Frankie thought, at least I did that for him, but it was a real nasty cut. I don't think I've ever seen a cut like that all the time I've been working here.

A cut like that should have a doctor.

The thought kept revolving in Frankie's mind. He knew that the cut was a bad one, he'd seen enough minor cuts to know that. And he knew that it should be treated by a doctor. And there was no reason now why it shouldn't have a doctor's care. Except one reason, and that was a big enough reason to keep Johnny away from any doctor in the city.

Johnny thought he was wanted for murder.

I should go to him, Frankie thought, I really should. I should go to him and tell him he's a free man.

But I can't.

I can't leave the drugstore, and even if I went on my lunch hour, I'd feel kind of silly about it. I mean, especially after having called the cops yesterday when he was here. I couldn't face him, not after that. Besides, I don't even know where he is.

Frankie fought the battle with himself right up to his lunch hour, and then he kept battling it out in his mind all the while he ate. When he went back to the drugstore, he still didn't know what to do. He knew Johnny should be told, but he also knew he could not bring himself to do the telling. He told himself he was not being cowardly. After all, he really didn't know where Johnny was. But in spite of what he told himself, he could not forget having called the cops on Johnny the day before, and he could not put the picture of that bleeding arm out of his mind. He worked listlessly, preoccupied, and Lefkowitz had to shout at him several times in order to get his attention back to his work.

When Hank Sands entered the drugstore, Frankie's problem was automatically solved.

He knew Sands, and he'd never liked him, but that didn't matter, not at the moment. Sands knew Harlem, and he knew everything about Harlem. What was more, he frequented the dive Cindy Matthews stripped in. Even if Sands didn't know where Johnny was, which was unlikely, he could pass the information on to Cindy, and she'd get it to Johnny. Frankie did not stop to wonder why he himself did not pass the information on to Cindy. He saw, in Hank Sands, a way out, and he seized it immediately.

He waited until Sands had made his small purchase, and then he said, "Hank, do you know where Johnny is?"

"Johnny who?" Sands said warily.

"Lane. Johnny Lane. Have you seen him?"

"Mebbe. Why you askin'?"

"I've got good news for him."

"Yeah? What kinda news?"

"The cops have caught Luis' killer. A guy named Charlie Brown. They're not looking for Johnny anymore. He's a free man."

"Yeah?" Sands considered this a moment, and his eyes narrowed. "How come you know this?"

"A cop was in here this morning. He told me."

"Yeah?"

"Yes. I thought you might get the information to Johnny. Or at least to Cindy. You could do that, couldn't you, Hank?"

"Cindy, huh?" Sands said. He weighed this carefully, and then he scratched his jaw. "You tell anybody else about this, Parker?"

"No, no one. You're the first one I saw who could help."

"Yeah," Sands said. "And you want me t'pass the word, that it? Get the word to Johnny." Sands paused. "Or Cindy."

"Yes."

"He a free man, that right?"

"Yes," Frankie said.

"But he don't know it." Sands smiled. "Pee-culiar situation, ain't it?"

"Reason I think he should find out fast, his arm is cut pretty bad."

"That right?" Sands asked.

"Yes."

"Then I s'pose Cindy—or Johnny—be mighty glad to get this piece of information. I mean, his arm bein' cut bad an' all."

"Yes. Can you take it to him, Hank?"

"Why, sure," Sands said, smiling. "Sure thing. Don't you worry 'bout it at all. I'll get on it right away."

"Well, thanks. That's a real load off my mind."

"Yeah," Sands said, smiling. The smile dropped from his face. "Now listen, man, don't you go telling this to nobody else, mind?"

"Why not?"

"I tell you why not. This thing starts spreadin' 'round Harlem, an' it'll assume the prop'ties of a rumor, you follow? You an intelligent cat, so you know what I mean. If ever'body talk about it, an' the rumble get back to Johnny, why, he won't know if'n it's true or not, follow?"

"Yes, I see what you mean."

"So you jus' keep your mouth tight on this, Parker. You tol' me, an' thass enough. I'll get the word to Johnny or Cindy, now don't you worry."

"Well, I certainly appreciate it, Hank."

"Don't mention it. I 'preciates the opportunity." Sands smiled and paid for his purchase. "Now, 'member, don't you go spoutin' over at the lip."

"I won't," Frankie promised.

"Me, I'm goan get started on this right now," Sands said. He nodded and smiled, and then walked to the door of the store and out onto the sidewalk. The sun was out now, and the day had turned into a very nice day, much warmer than the day before, an almost Indian-summer day. Sands breathed deeply of the mild air, and the smile grew on his face. Without hesitation, he headed for Cindy's apartment.

The sunlight struck his closed eyes, spreading a violent orange onto his eyeballs. He did not know how long the orange color had been there, but it startled him into wakefulness, and he sat upright abruptly, opening his eyes.

He did not know where he was for a moment, and he stared around the room in puzzlement while awareness seeped slowly into his mind. His body was tense on the bed until he identified the room, and then he visibly relaxed and sighed. Cindy's place.

And then he remembered that Cindy had been in the bed with him, and he glanced quickly at the pillow beside him, seeing the indentation of her head there. He felt the sheets quickly, and they were cold where Cindy had lain.

"Cindy?" he called.

He listened, his ears automatically blocking out the street noises below. He could hear every sound in the apartment; the ticking of the white-faced clock on the dresser, the steady tap-tap of the water faucet in the bathroom, the clanking of the radiators.

"Cindy?" he called again.

When he got no answer, he swung his legs over the side of the bed and looked around the room. Cindy's pajama top was on the floor where she'd dropped it. He remembered seeing her clothing folded over the back of the chair last night, and when he looked at the chair now, the clothing was gone, except for a pair of panties and nylon stockings, which she'd probably changed today. The stockings looked peculiarly forlorn without Cindy's legs inside them. He picked one up, feeling the nylon as it trailed over his fingers, remembering Cindy's body again, remembering a little of last night.

Had he fallen asleep?

That was rich. Chalk up a first for Johnny Lane. He'd fallen asleep with a girl like Cindy beside him. He smiled, and then the smile evaporated when he remembered that Cindy wasn't in the apartment now.

He called, "Cindy!" again, just to check, and then he went into the small bathroom, even looking in the tub. No, she wasn't in the apartment. Then where was she? He scratched his head.

At the club?

What the hell time was it, anyway?

He walked to the dresser and picked the clock up. Twelve-thirty, and the clock ran ten minutes fast, so that made it twelve-twenty. He'd slept for about four or five hours, he supposed. He felt completely refreshed. Aside from the damned throbbing in his arm, he felt like a new man. Cindy would be surprised to see him looking so good.

But where the hell was she?

Twelve-twenty. What does a girl do at twelve-twenty?

He put the clock back on the dresser, and then scanned the apartment. He stood in his underwear, the T shirt very white against his dark skin, and when he spotted the note propped up against the coffeepot, he crossed the room with long strides. The pot was on the stove, set against one end of the combination kitchen-bedroom, alongside the icebox. He picked up the note, unfolded it, and read it hastily:

> Johnny dear:
>   I went down for some groceries and the newspaper. If you should wake up before I come back, there is coffee in the pot, just heat it, and some buns in the breadbox on top of the icebox. I washed the blood out of your shirt (did you know the bottom was all torn?) and ironed it. It's hanging in the bathroom on a hanger. I love you.
>   CINDY

He felt the smile come onto his face, and he read the note through again, smiling all the while. He folded the note then and took it to the dresser, and after he'd pulled on his pants, he put the note in his pocket. He found the broken orange-crate stick in his back pocket, and he held it on the palm of his hand and thought, I won't need this any more. Not with Cindy to take care of me.

He kept thinking of the note and smiling. He carried the stick to the garbage pail and was ready to throw it in when he saw that the pail wasn't lined. He looked around the apartment, spotting the newspaper on the table. He walked to it and then realized he hadn't seen a paper since he started running. He'd bought a paper when he needed change to call Cindy, but he'd thrown that away without opening it. He wondered now if the paper carried the story of Luis' death, and he scanned it rapidly.

There was nothing, but that didn't surprise him. A guy gets zip-gunned in Harlem. So what? Nothing to start fussing about. He took three pages from the newspaper, went back to the garbage pail, lined it, and then dumped the stick into it, feeling like a man launching a battleship.

Damn if he didn't feel good today! He couldn't wait to tell Cindy how he felt, he couldn't wait for her to get back to the apartment. He'd tell her all about it, and then later he'd take to the streets again, wearing Barney's coat, and damn if he wouldn't find Luis' killer.

That was real nice of her, he thought abruptly. Washing and ironing my shirt. He walked into the bathroom, where the hanger rested on a nail in the wall. He took down the shirt and smelled it, and he smiled again and then put it on, rolling the sleeves a few inches above his wrists and leaving the collar unbuttoned.

It must be like this when you're married, he thought. Clean shirts all the time, and a woman like Cindy. I should marry her. I really should marry her, but I have to get a good job first, and then she can quit working in the Yahoo. Hell of a thing for a man's wife to be stripping for every jerk who can afford a drink. No, that's for the sparrows. I'll get a good job once this is all over, and then me and Cindy will tie the knot, and then she can stop undressing in public, providing I can get a good job.

Well, he'd try. You can't stop a man from trying, that's for sure. But first he'd have to clear up all this stinking mess. You can't get a job, good or otherwise, when the cops are after you. Well, today he'd start asking some questions, sniff around a little. He felt a lot better today, except for the throbbing, and today he'd turn cop. Like "Harlem Detective" on TV. Now, there was a good show. Why in hell had they dropped it?

He walked to the stove, struck a match, and lighted the flame beneath the coffeepot. He found a cup and saucer in the cabinet over the range, and then he took the buns from the breadbox and brought them to the table. When the coffee was hot, he poured a cup and sat at the table to drink it, black. It was curious how he wasn't hungry anymore. He supposed his stomach had shrunk or something.

Where was Cindy?

He wanted her to come back to the apartment very badly. He felt very strong, but he also felt very lonely, and it seemed as if she'd been gone for ten years. He wanted to see her again. He wanted to sit at the table with her and share a pot of coffee, and then he'd tell her about everything that had happened to him, and she'd listen with her face tilted a little bit, with the lipstick on her mouth and just that faint touch of rouge on each cheek. She had good bones, Cindy, a good face. And her eyes were very nice. Her whole face paid close attention when you talked to her, and her eyes especially. He wanted to talk to her and feel her eyes on him while he talked. When you talked to Cindy, she made you feel like you were the only person in the world, but where the hell was she now?

He swallowed the hot coffee and then nibbled at one of the buns. The bun was stale, but that wasn't her fault. She wasn't expecting company.

He smiled at that. The man who came to dinner. How long would he have to stay here at Cindy's place? Would the cops come back? Wouldn't it be a hell of a thing if they caught him before he had a chance to see her again? Suppose the goddamn cops came to get him, and fried him, and he never saw Cindy again? And then, twenty years later, the bastard who shot Luis would come to the police and confess, and Molly would sue the city and the state for eight million dollars, but that still wouldn't do him any good. He'd be dead and buried, six feet under, and he wouldn't ever have seen Cindy again, and when you're dead, you're dead, man.

The thought began to plague his mind until it became almost a reality. Come on, Cindy, he pleaded. Come home, baby.

When the knock sounded on the door, he leaped to his feet instantly, whirling.

"Cindy?" he asked.

There was a brief hesitation on the other side of the door, and he wondered for a panicky moment if there were cops out there. He waited breathlessly, and then the voice came after what seemed a very long time.

"No. That you, Johnny?"

He recognized the voice. Hank Sands. He felt relieved until he realized Sands could be as dangerous as the cops, and then he debated opening the door. There was no sense in keeping it closed now. Sands knew he was here.

"Just a minute," he said.

He crossed to the door and opened it quickly.

"Come in," he said. "Fast."

Sands smiled and stepped into the apartment. He looked at the rumpled bed, and his smile got bigger.

" 'Lo, Johnny," he said. "Didn't 'spec to find you here."

"Then what are you doing here?" Johnny asked.

"Oh, jus' thought I'd pass the time o' day with Cindy. No harm in that, is there?" He paused and looked around the apartment again. "She . . . uh . . . gone?"

"Yes," Johnny said.

"Mmmm." Sands nodded. "Say, I see you got some coffee there. Mind?"

"Help yourself," Johnny said.

Sands looked around until he spotted the cabinet. He walked to it, took down a cup and saucer, and then brought them back to the table. He lifted the coffeepot from the table and shook his head.

"Shun't do that, man, leave a hot pot on a wooden

table. Liable'a burn a hole." He poured his cup full and then asked, "You want another cup, Johnny?"

"All right," Johnny said.

Sands poured and then carried the pot back to the stove. "I see sugar on the table," he said, "but no milk. In the icebox?"

"I suppose," Johnny answered. The idea of Sands' coming to see Cindy annoyed the hell out of him.

Sands rummaged in the icebox and came up with a half-full bottle of milk. He brought this to the table and sat opposite Johnny.

"Why'd you come here, Sands?" Johnny asked.

Sands opened his eyes wide. "Me? Well, like I tol' you. Jus' to pass the time o' day with Cindy."

"She wouldn't pass *wind* with you, Sands. Why'd you come?"

"Man, I never see such a distrustful cat. I tol' you, boy."

"Did you know I was here?"

Sands considered this gravely. "Well, now, I wun't say that."

"Did you know I was here, Sands?"

"Not 'zactly. I mean, the rumble is out, but—"

"What rumble?"

Sands smiled. "Man, they a big search out for you. Didn't you know that?"

"Of course I knew it! Why the hell do you think— But what rumble? What do you mean, the rumble's out?"

"Well, way I got it, the cops figure you to be one o' two places. Either here or up with Molly."

"Who told you that, Sands?"

"Oh, you hear things."

Sands sipped at his coffee and then put down the cup. He reached for a bun, bit into it, pulled a sour face, and dropped it to the table.

"Where'd you hear it, Sands?"

"Oh, around."

"Any cops downstairs when you came up?"

"Nary a one. Now, doan let me worry you, boy. I

jus' sayin' what I heard, thass all. Now, there ain' no need to get excited."

"If the cops think I'm here, why haven't they come after me?"

"Now, I wouldn't know, Johnny, and thass the truth. I jus' sayin' what the rumble was, thass all."

"You sure there were no cops downstairs?"

"I'm sure, boy. I wun't a come up if there hadda been."

Johnny considered what Sands had just told him. If the cops figured him to be here, why hadn't they closed in yet? The problem bothered him.

" 'Course," Sands said, "they figger you to be pretty dang'rous, way I got it. Maybe they waitin' for reinforcements or sutthin'."

"Dangerous? Me? Are you kidding?"

"Hell, Johnny, you *did* kill a man, you know," Sands said, seemingly offended.

"I told you I didn't kill nobody. Whoever killed Luis is still out there someplace, laughing himself sick."

Sands smiled. "Is he, now?"

"Yes, he is," Johnny said angrily. "That sonovabitch. If I had him here, I'd—"

"Well, too bad the cops ain' hip to the situation," Sands said. "Too bad they lookin' for the wrong man, eh, boy?"

"You trying to rub it in, Sands?"

"No, no, hell, no. I jus' tryin' to recap, you know. I tryin' to 'splain the setup to you, thass all, Johnny. Things don't look too good fum where I sit."

"Shut up, Sands. I can see the picture without you explaining it."

"I on'y tryin' to help out, man."

"You can help out by shutting the hell up."

"Sure," Sands said. He smiled and sipped at his coffee again. "You . . . uh . . . spend the night here, Johnny?"

"Why?"

"I jus' askin'."

"Yes, I did."

"Mmmmm," Sands said, lifting his eyebrows and rolling his eyes.

"Look, Sands . . ."

"Cindy gone now, huh? She comin' back soon?"

"What business is that of yours?"

"Jus' thought I might say hello. No need to get upset, Johnny."

"I don't want you saying hello to her, Sands."

"Well, now, a man in your position, the cops after him an' all, now that ain' a nice way to talk. Man, that dragnet gettin' tighter and tighter all the time."

"Shut up, Sands."

" 'F I was you, Johnny, I'd cut out o' here. Now I know you like Cindy an' all that, but man, those cops ain' kiddin', you know? 'Sides, if you really cared 'bout her, you wouldn't want to get her in trouble, now would you?"

"What do you mean?"

"Well, it sure ain' goan look good for her when the cops find you here, now is it?"

Johnny didn't answer. He pulled at his lip and blinked his eyes.

"I think you should cut out, man," Sands said. "Thass what I think."

"Maybe you should be the one cuttin' out," Johnny answered.

Sands smiled broadly, "Thass a nice way to talk, all right. Man comes here and wises you up on the situation, an' you talk to him like that."

"You didn't tell me nothing I didn't already know."

"You din't know the cops figured you to be here, did you?"

"Well, that I didn't know."

"Well, man, now you know it."

"Thanks."

"Doan mention it. You gonna cut out?"

"Why?"

"I jus' askin'."

"Maybe," Johnny said.

"Thass the smart thing t'do. No sense gettin' Cindy in a jam, too."

"I suppose not," Johnny said. "You better go now, Sands."

"O.K.," Sands said. He rose and buttoned the top button of his heavy overcoat. "Johnny, I sure as hell is sorry you went and killed Luis. I—"

"I didn't kill that bastard!" Johnny shouted. "How many times do I have to tell you that? My God, Sands, you're enough to—"

"Now easy, boy, easy. I jus' sayin' what I heard, thass all. An' I *am* sorry you in trouble. You need any help, you jus' call on me, Johnny."

"Yeah."

"No, I mean it."

"Sure. You'll probably go right to the cops the second you leave here."

"Me? Man, you think *I'd* do a thing like that?" Sands looked hurt. "I on'y got your interests at heart, Johnny."

"I'll bet. Cut out, Sands."

Sands walked to the door. "See you, boy."

He unlocked the door and stepped out into the hallway. Johnny rose from the table, walked to the door, and locked it again. He wasn't at all sure that Sands would not go to the cops. Especially since he'd said the cops already figured him to be here. It would be just like that sonovabitch to turn him in.

And even if he didn't, there was no sense staying here any longer. Sands had been right about that, anyway. It would only get Cindy in trouble, and he didn't want that. He'd have to leave.

The thought galled him because he'd really wanted to see Cindy again. He'd barely talked to her last night before he corked off, and he was annoyed that he wouldn't get a chance to talk to her now. He shoved the thought out of his mind. He stalled around for a few minutes, hoping she might show up, and then he realized he was just stalling, and he looked for a pencil and then took Cindy's note from his pocket.

On the bottom of the note he scribbled: "Cops may come, honey. I'll get in touch with you. J."

He put the note against the sugar bowl on the table, sighed, and then shrugged into Barney Knowles's overcoat.

When he reached the street, he did not see Hank Sands standing in the hallway across the street, watching him leave.

Chapter Eleven

If you looked hard, you could see the Empire State Building down there, and the other tall one, that was the Chrysler Building. And you could see bridges from up here, too, and all the rivers that hemmed in Manhattan. You could see the Triboro, and the Queensborough, and on the other side the George Washington, which was his favorite bridge. The rivers looked like snakes from up here, and if you listened hard, you could hear the lonesome sound of the tugs sometimes, and once in a while one of the big liners going down the Hudson.

Most of all, you could see Harlem.

You could see all of Harlem stretched out at your feet, spreading down there below you. You could see Harlem, and you could feel it, feel the vibration of Harlem under the rooftops, almost taste Harlem.

It was warm up there on the roof. The day had turned mild, and the sun had scattered the dismal fog of early morning. It was almost spring up there on the roof, and he breathed the air deeply and forgot for the first time that he was running. He could see Cindy's building from where he stood, and he could also see his own building, and he could pick out other spots that he knew by the roofs alone. Johnny Lane was not a stranger to rooftops.

They spread out below him in a crazy vertical and horizontal patchwork quilt. Black and brown and tan, like the people of Harlem. And white sheets flapping from clotheslines, and the white was fitting, too, because there were white men in Harlem, among the black and the brown and the tan.

There was something very tranquil about rooftops.

He used to go up on the roof of his own building a lot when he was a little kid. He used to go up on the roof then only to lean on a skylight maybe and look out over Harlem and think about things.

When he got a little older, the roof began to mean other things to him. The roof meant a place to take a girl. You could always take a girl up to the roof, usually at night, but sometimes even during the day. It was best at night, with the stars making a big canopy up there, and the neons tinting the horizon, and the jukes going strong in all the bars along the avenue. You spread a blanket out, and then you lay side by side, and the girl's flesh was always cool somehow, even on the hottest summer nights when the roof couldn't escape the pent-up city heat. You usually got chased. If somebody stumbled up there and caught you, he screamed like a bastard, and you had to run, but that didn't matter because there were other roofs and other girls, but still you didn't like to run, it was kind of embarrassing for the girl.

And sometimes the roof was a sanctuary. You ran up there whenever one of the guys pulled a purse snatch. You ran up there after you swiped a stick of gum from a candy counter. You ran up there after you hit a bar with a pail, had it filled with beer, making out it was for your old man, and then cut out without paying for the pail. You ran up there with the other guys, and you drank it, and it tasted better because you'd swiped it. A guy could cross all of Harlem, practically, by taking to the rooftops, and it was senseless to chase you up there. The roofs were real good for running, and there was a lot of running when he was growing up.

You ran up there whenever you were chased. Once when the Golden Guardians had come down from 144th Street, all carrying knives and broken bottles, he and the other kids had taken to the roofs and stayed up there all day. They'd gone up to the roofs the second time the GG's raided their block, too. Only this time they'd gone up there with rocks and bricks and empty gallon jugs, and they'd given it to the GG's right from the rooftops, throwing it all down on them, splitting a few skulls like they did in the old times when there were knights and besieged castles. One of the bricks had hit an old lady, too, and fractured her skull, and when the bulls showed, they'd all run like bastards over the rooftops until they were far away from the block. The bulls knew the rooftops, but they never chased you up there unless it was real serious. They knew you could run faster than they could because you'd had a lot of practice at it. And they also knew you knew the roofs better than they did, so there was no sense in a prolonged chase.

When you got hip to tea, you used the roof for another purpose. You drifted up there with a bunch of the boys, and maybe sometimes a chick or two in the crowd. You handed out the reefers, or maybe a goofball or two, or sometimes even a sniff of C. And then you just lay back and blew your cork. The high was the end, man, because it took you away from everything down there, and you weren't running from anything, you were just sort of floating around, and sometimes the chicks helped you float. Sometimes you got caught when you were high, and then you were running again. This was serious stuff, and the cops chased you on this serious stuff, even if they didn't know the roofs as good as you did.

You did a lot of running in Harlem.

Most of all, you tried to run away from the fact that you were black and most everybody else in the world was white. He knew most of the chicks used skin bleaches, and even some of the guys he knew used them, though they didn't much talk about it. And there were hair-straighteners, and he'd heard of black men passing as whites for years, but he didn't go for none of that crap, he didn't want to change the color of his skin or the kinkiness of his hair, he didn't want that at all.

He just wanted to be . . . somebody. Something. A person. In Harlem, in his home, in the place where his roots ran deep, he was a person. But once he stepped outside of Harlem, once he went down to a movie in Times Square, or a ball game at the stadium, or anything like that, anything that took him away from Harlem, he became painfully conscious of the color of his skin.

He had never met a white man with whom he could be comfortable. He tried to tell himself that he was being stupid, that not all white men looked at his skin first and then the rest of him, but he could not believe himself. He still remembered the beating he'd got that time in Wop Harlem when a white girl stopped to ask him for a match. He'd lighted her cigarette for her, and his mind told everyone he was just performing a courtesy, just lighting a cigarette for a stranger who didn't happen to have a match.

But his skin was saying another thing entirely. His skin was telling everybody that he was annoying this white girl, and all the wops came off their stoops with chairs and beer bottles and whatever they could get their hands on, and they proceeded to beat the hell out of him.

Later, when he had a chance to think about it, he did not blame the wops at all. He knew that a white man in Harlem would be running the same risk if he got friendly with a colored girl, unless he did it on the Market, where it was for sale, and some colored guys didn't even like whites doing it there.

So he blamed the skin. It was all the skin's fault, and a white man's skin in Harlem lied just as much as a black man's skin outside of Harlem.

And so while Johnny Lane knew the sensible thing to do, he ignored it. The sensible thing to do was go to the cops. The sensible thing to do was show them that he could not possibly have had anything to do with the killing of Luis.

That was the sensible thing. But Johnny remembered the words of the cop when they'd argued near the park bench on the Golden Edge.

"What're you wastin' time arguing with a nigger for?"

Maybe the cop meant nothing by it. Maybe the cop was just one of those white men who automatically, through training or exposure or both, called all Negroes "niggers." Maybe so. Maybe his use of the word had meant nothing at all. Maybe he was anxious to get this thing over with, anxious to get a cup of coffee or something, who the hell knows or cares?

The word was a bullet aimed at him, and the word ricocheted there inside, and the answering word was *run!*

He'd run, and he was still running.

And as he stood on the rooftop now, looking down at the Harlem he loved and hated, hearing the sounds below him hushed by early winter, feeling the mildness of a day that was anything but winter, another thought came to him, and his brow furrowed for a moment, and then his eyes got a little cloudy.

For Johnny Lane had just realized with sudden clarity that he'd actually been running all his life.

The bar on Seventh Avenue was set right next door to a store-front church, and Hank Sands could hear the congregation singing next door as he sat at the bar and toyed with a jigger of rye.

He stared into the small amber eye of the glass thoughtfully, and then twirled it between his thumb and forefinger. Expertly he lifted the glass and tossed off the shot, and then he made an "Ahhh" sound and wiped his lips. The liquor traveled down to his gut, and he felt it nestling there, warm and glowing. He had really needed that shot.

He thought of Cindy Matthews again, and a smile formed on his face. Cindy Matthews, the snootiest broad he knew. Always with the cold shoulder, always treating him like dirt. Except now he had what she wanted, and brother, was she going to pay for it! And let Johnny Lane try to stop it. Just let him try.

The smile expanded unconsciously, a pleased smile

that covered half his face. Abe, the bartender, strolled over to where Sands was sitting.

"You care for another, Hank?" he asked.

"No," Sands said, still smiling. "No, thass quite enough. I had quite enough, thank you."

"Strange t' see you in here so early, Hank," Abe said.

Sands' smile turned into a secret one. "Got a big deal cookin'."

"Oh, that right?"

"Thass right. Got to close this deal in a little while, so I figgered I'd grab a pick-me-up first."

"Sensible idea," Abe said, nodding. "Have another, Hank."

"No, no, I need a clear head for this deal."

"Important stuff huh?" Abe asked.

"Man," Sands said, chuckling, "this is the most importantest stuff I can think of. This is a deal I been dyin' to close for a long time now, Abe. Funny thing, I never thought I *would* get to close this deal, y'know what I mean?"

"Didn't have the money, that it, Hank?"

"No, money didn't enter into this deal a-tall, Abe. No, that wun't no consideration. Wun't money holdin' me back, nossir."

"What then, Hank?"

"Well, le's say I lacked the bargaining tools, Abe. Le's say that."

"And you got those now, huh?"

Sands couldn't hold back the chuckle. "Man, have I got the bargaining tools now! Man, have I got them! Never was a man with such bargainin' power, believe me, Abe."

"Well, good. I like to see a man get ahead," Abe said seriously. "Me, I guess I'll always be a bartender."

"You jus' got to look for your opportunity and grab it," Sands said. He held both hands out in front of him, as if he were weighing the air, and then he suddenly clenched his fingers. "Jus' grab it, tha's all."

"You going to close the deal this afternoon?"

"I am," Sands said. "I am that. An' you know sutthin', Abe? I goan enjoy this. I really goan enjoy it."

"It's important for a man to like his work," Abe said glumly.

"Oh, I goan like this work, all right. This the work I was cut out for." Sands chuckled again, and Abe looked at him quizzically. "Say, what time's it?" Sands asked.

Abe looked at his watch. "Almost one-thirty," he said.

"My party might be back by now," Sands said. "I better run 'long. I sure don't want to miss out on this." He nodded his head. "No, not after all that waitin'." He slid off the bar stool and paid for his drink.

"Well, so long, Abe. I'll be seein' you."

Abe smiled and waved. "Good luck, man."

Sands walked out of the bar and past the store front next door. He could hear the congregation praying inside, their voices rising in unison. No amount of prayin's gonna help Cindy, he thought. No amount of prayin' at all.

He walked with a brisk stride, enjoying the way the day had changed, enjoying the mildness of the air. There were a lot of people in the streets now, and he watched the women and the young girls go by, and he smiled unconsciously because he saw Cindy Matthews in every woman he passed. It was almost like spring, and as Sands walked he felt this overpowering love for every woman he saw, this feeling that he actually loved each and every one of them, that he could see beauty in the ugliest woman who passed, but not a beauty like Cindy's, and still he could love each and every one of them, he could see in each something that some man, somewhere, could love.

He was surprised to find himself thinking this way, because love did not enter into his plans at all. He was honest enough to admit that. He did not love Cindy Matthews, nor had he ever entertained such high-flown ideas about her.

He had thought about her often, yes. He had first

111

spotted her when she was just a kid first flowering into womanhood, the straight lines of her body yielding to soft curves. He had watched her walk down the street, a snooty little thing even then, with her nose high in the air, and her small pointed breasts showing under the thin dress because she was still too young to wear a brassiere. He had watched her a good deal, but he hadn't made any move because she was still just a kid, and he didn't want trouble.

And then, all of a sudden, she wasn't a kid any more. She was a stripper at the Yahoo, and he went there often to watch her undress. He tried to be nice about this one. He played up to her, and he smiled, but she always cut him dead. She preferred Johnny Lane, a young snotnose, how old could he be, twenty-one, twenty-two? It had irked him. He had wanted her very badly, and the want had expanded in his mind until it became almost a thing of hatred, until he'd thought many times of taking her by force.

Until this better way had come along. Until Frankie Parker had dropped this better way right into his lap, and oh, what a honey this better way was! What a lovely little honey Frankie Parker had given him!

He turned left on 142nd Street and walked directly to Cindy's building. He tried to be casual about it, but the excitement flared within him, and he found his hands trembling as he mounted the steps to the stoop. He went into the hallway, and then began climbing the inside steps. He was breathing hard, and he knew it wasn't from the climb, but that would be all over soon, all of it.

He reached her doorway and knocked.

He heard a rustle inside, and he wondered for a moment what she'd be wearing. This was almost like going to the Market, except better, because he didn't have to pay anything for it, and Cindy was a hundred times better than any slut on the Market.

"Who is it?" she asked from behind the closed door.

"Me," he said. "Hank."

"Oh." Her voice sounded disappointed. The bitch

was probably expecting Johnny back. Well, Johnny was gone now. He'd waited downstairs until he saw him leave, and then he'd gone to the bar for his shot. Johnny was gone, and now there were just the two of them, and that juicy piece of information, that big bargaining tool.

"What do you want, Hank?" Cindy asked.

"I got some news for you, Cindy," he said. Careful now, he warned himself. Don't go spilling it. It's not a tool if you let it out before you get what you want.

"What kind of news?" she asked suspiciously.

"God, can'tcha open the door even?" he said.

"All right, just a minute."

She opened the door, and his eyes roamed her body candidly. She was wearing a skirt and a silk blouse, and the blouse was unbuttoned at the throat, and his eyes fled to the deep valley between her breasts. Her hand went to her throat self-consciously, covering the cleft.

"What is it, Hank?"

"Let me in, Cindy. This is important news."

Cindy looked extremely disturbed, and she glanced off down the hallway and then said, "You'll have to make this fast."

"Why, sure," he lied, "sure." He stepped into the apartment and then went to the table, taking off his coat and sitting.

"Don't make yourself too comfortable," Cindy said.

"Got to be comfy to give news," Hank said.

"What's your news?"

"Now, ain't you goan offer me some coffee?"

"What's your news, Hank?"

"This news, honey, this news is sutthin' I think might interest you," he said. "Now, whatcha think might interest you?"

"I don't know," she said warily.

"Well, now, think. Think hard."

She stared at him levelly, and he saw that she was beginning to understand. She was beginning to realize he wasn't going to tell her right away. She was a smart girl, and she read that in his eyes, and he saw her reading it.

"I can't think of any news," she said. "What is it?"

"Aw, now, you ain' half tryin', Cindy."

"What is it, Hank? Are you going to tell me?"

"Why, sure I am. Thass what I come here for, Cindy, to bring you this news."

"Then what is it?"

"I ast you to try an' guess, now din't I? Well, I doan hear you guessin' none, Cindy."

"Is . . . is it about Johnny?" she asked.

"Well, now, thass a pretty good guess, Cindy girl. Yes, I'd say it was about Johnny. Now, how about a cup o' coffee, honey? I sure could use a—"

"What about Johnny? Is he hurt? Have they caught him?"

"Now, now, now," Sands chided. "Now, now, le's have that coffee first, an' then we'll see about me tellin' you."

"Is he hurt? For God's sake, Hank!"

"The coffee," Sands said.

"Can't you even—" She looked at his face, and then cut herself short. "All right. All right, I'll get you some coffee." She walked to the range, and he watched the skirt tighten across her buttocks, watched the way the long slit starting at the hem revealed her calves when she walked. She was wearing high-heeled shoes, and he looked at the shoes and then said, "Why don't you take off them shoes, Cindy?"

She glanced down at the shoes, and then turned to light the gas under the coffeepot. "What for?"

"I like 'em better off. I like a girl walkin' 'round the apartment without her shoes on." Sands paused. "Makes a girl look sexy 'thout her shoes on, Cindy."

She shook out the match and then turned to face him again, a puzzled look in her eyes. "I think I'll leave them on," she said firmly.

"Why, sure, do what you want." Sands sighed heavily. "Guess I'll be runnin' along, Cindy. Don't want to keep you."

"You said you had some news."

"Why, sure. Sure I got news. An' I'm the on'y cat in Harlem got this news, an' this news concerns Johnny, it do. But a man asks someone t' take off her shoes, an' she acks like he's poison or sutthin'. Well, Cindy, I guess I knows when I ain't wanted, I guess I can see that, all right."

He made a motion to rise, and Cindy said, "Stay put, Hank."

He watched her as she shoved one shoe off her foot, using the other foot to loosen it. She stepped out of the second shoe then, and he looked at her painted toenails inside the sheer nylons, and he felt the tremor start in his hands again. He clenched his hands on the table and forced a smile. If he got her to take off her shoes, he'd get her to do anything. This was going along fine. This was going along just the way he wanted it to go along.

"My shoes are off," she said.

"Yeah, I can see that. You got nice legs, Cindy, real nice legs. Shame they all hidden most of the time. 'Cept at the Yahoo, an' there ain't much hidden there, now is there?"

"Tell me about Johnny," she said. "Have the police got him? Is that the news?"

"No, that ain' it, Cindy, but don't ask me nothin' else till I got my coffee in me. I can't talk straight 'thout havin' my coffee. Whyn't you sit down, girl?"

"I'm all right standing," she said.

"Go on, Cindy," Sands said softly. "Sit down."

She looked at him again, and he looked back at her this time, and again he sensed she saw something on his face. Her eyes widened a little. She took a look at the coffeepot, and then walked over to the table, sitting quietly, her feet flat on the floor.

"Now, you should cross your legs when you sit, Cindy honey," Sands said. "More comfortable that way."

"I'm comfortable," she said. She kept looking at him curiously.

"You be more comfortable if'n you cross them, Cindy," he said.

"Look, Hank, what is this? Have you got something to tell me or are you just—"

"Now doan get me upset, Cindy. You get me upset, an' I liable'a walk clear out o' here 'thout tellin' you what I know. Now, you don't want that to happen, do you?"

"No. But if you think—"

"If I think *what*, Cindy?"

"Well, I don't know what you're thinking."

"I'm jus' thinkin' you should cross them legs o' yours, Cindy, 'cause you'll be more comfortable that way. Tha's the only thing I'm thinkin' right now."

Cindy drew in a deep breath, and his eyes fled to the front of her blouse. She let out the breath quickly.

"Don't you think it'll be more comfy?" Sands asked.

"I . . . I guess so," she said. She crossed her legs quickly and then reached for her hem, moving to pull the skirt down over her knees.

"No," Sands said, "leave it just like that."

Cindy uncrossed her legs and rose angrily. "The hell with this!" she said. "I'll be damned if I'm going to—" She saw the smile on Sands' face and cut herself off. "Get out of here, Hank. I don't need your news."

"Ah, but you do," Sands said, smiling. "I'm the on'y cat what knows it. An' it's damn important, Cindy. Say, ain' that coffee ready yet?"

She walked to the stove in her stocking feet, and he listened to the slap of her feet against the linoleum, wetting his lips. He had to be careful about this. He didn't want to lose it, and she'd almost slipped off the hook then. He had to give her a little more.

"Now, listen here to me, Cindy," he said. "I ain' snowin' you, girl. This is important. It's important to you, an' it's important to Johnny, mighty important to Johnny. So stop actin' like a prima donna, an' simmer down an' listen. You hear?"

"I hear," Cindy said from the stove.

"Then hear good, and don't go insultin' me, neither,

'cause I'll walk out o' here sure as you're standin' there, an' then you an' Johnny can go plumb to hell both. I'm doin' you a favor as it is, comin' here to tell you this."

"You said the police didn't get him?"

"They ain't got him. I wun't come here to tell you that."

"Then he's hurt. Is that it? He's hurt and he needs my help?"

"Le's have the coffee, Cindy."

Cindy bit her lip, and then brought the coffee and a cup and saucer to the table. She poured the coffee for Sands, and then took the pot back to the stove, returning with a bottle of milk. Sands poured a little milk into the coffee, put two teaspoonfuls of sugar into it, and then sipped at it.

"Mmm," he said, "this is real good coffee, Cindy. You make a nice cup of coffee."

"*Is* he hurt, Hank? Is that what you came to tell me?"

"Well, you know 'bout his arm, don't you, Cindy?"

"Yes. Has it started bleed—"

"Cindy, I do wish you'd sit down an' cross them pretty legs of yours. I like watchin' them legs o' yours when they crossed. I mean, for a girl who shows her navel every night, you sure persnickety 'bout showin' a li'l knee to an old friend got information for you."

"All right, all right, all right," Cindy said impatiently. She crossed her legs rapidly, leaving the skirt above her knees. Sands looked at her knees and smiled. He moved his chair a little closer to hers.

"You *do* know 'bout the arm then, huh?"

"Is that all this is about? Is that what you—"

"Cindy, this the most important information I ever had to d'liver. This information can mean Johnny's life, an' I ain't snowin' you."

"Has he started bleeding again?"

"Cindy," Sands said slowly, "take off your clothes."

She stared at him as if she hadn't heard him.

"What?" she said.

117

"I'd like to look at your legs, Cindy. I'd 'preciate it if you took off your clothes."

"What?" she said again, stunned. "What?"

The smile dropped from Sands' face. "I want you to take off your clothes," he said. "I want you to take them off right now, right this minute. An' then we'll see about tellin' you this information."

"Is that what you want?" she said. "Just that?"

Sands smiled again. "No. Not just that."

"You must be crazy," she said.

"You got a choice, Cindy," Sands told her.

"I thought so. From the second you came in here."

"You can either—"

"No. The answer is no. Get out of here before I vomit. Get out of here before I—"

"You can either kick me out," Sands persisted, "or you can hear me out. If you hear me out, considerin' Johnny's bad arm an' all, you can likely save his life. He's out there someplace, you know."

"No," Cindy said. "Get out."

"Sure," Sands answered, smiling. He got up and put on his coat. "He's your boy friend, not mine."

"How do I know this information is the goods? How do I know you're not lying just to—just to get what you want?"

"You got to take my word, honey. You ain't got a choice."

"Your word is about as good as—"

"Take it or leave it. Yes or no?" Sands said tightly.

"How do I know you'll tell me after . . . afterward?"

He could see it was gnawing at her. He could see the idea didn't appeal to her, but she sure as hell wanted this news. She bit her lip and stared at him worriedly.

"You got to take my word," he repeated.

She seemed to consider for a long time. Sands shrugged, figuring it was now or never. He had to force her hand, and there was only one way to do that.

"Well, honey," he said, "you done had your chance. I'll see you 'round."

He went to the door and put his hand on the door-knob. He started to open the door.

"Wait," Cindy said softly.

Sands turned and looked at her expectantly.

"Sit down," she said. And then, in almost a whisper, "I'll . . . I'll do what you want."

Sands took off his coat and sat down on the edge of the bed. Cindy looked at him again, and he saw the disgust on her face, and somehow the disgust pleased him immensely.

"Go on," he said. "I'm waitin'."

She pulled the blouse out of her skirt and began unbuttoning it. She folded the blouse over a chair, working like an automaton. She unhooked her skirt and then pulled down the zipper, letting it fall to her feet and stepping out of it. She took off her stockings, and then she hesitated, and Sands looked at her again, and she seemed to decide that hesitation was the wrong thing with him watching her. He leaned forward anxiously now, feeling the heat at the pit of his stomach, watching her uncover her body. She undressed rapidly, and then she stood naked near the stove, looking at him hesitantly, trembling a little.

Sands smiled and stuck his hands out in front of him, as if he were weighing the air.

"Come here, baby," he said.

She got out of bed immediately afterward. She lighted a cigarette to take the taste of his foul kisses out of her mouth, and then she threw on a robe and crossed her arms over it. She felt filthy. She had never felt like this before, never in her life. Even the first time, and she'd been forced that time, even then she had not felt this filthy.

"Tell me," she said. She did not look at him. She kept her back to him, not wanting to see him as he dressed.

"Tell you what?" Sands asked.

She whirled rapidly. "You said—"

"The news, you mean? Oh, the information. That what you want me to tell you?"

"Yes. What is it about Johnny?"

Sands dressed quickly. "I tell you, honey," he said, pulling his jacket on, "I tell you, I really enjoyed that. I sure did."

"For God's sake," she shouted, "is Johnny hurt?"

Sands buttoned his jacket and put on his coat. "I really liked it. I think I'll come back for more tomorrow."

"What?" She looked at him, stunned.

"Or maybe tonight. Maybe I'll stop by tonight, Cindy, an' we'll see about it then, huh, Cindy?"

"You . . . you didn't have anything to tell me!" she said, shocked with the realization. "It was all a trick!"

"I got something," he said, "an' maybe I'll tell it to you tonight. I'll stop by 'fore you go to the club, Cindy."

She stared at him for a moment, and then she said, "Oh, you rotten sonovabitch."

She flung herself across the room, tossing away the cigarette, her fingers spread wide. Her nails caught at the flesh under his eyes, and she pulled downward with all her strength, feeling the skin rip. She clawed higher, wanting to get at his eyes, wanting to rip the bastard's eyes out. Her nails raked his forehead, tore his nose, and she heard him scream like a woman. He turned his head, and then he brought his hand up in a sharp punch that caught her on the chest. She staggered backward and he went after her, hitting her again, still with a bunched fist, catching her on the mouth this time. She fell to the floor, tasting the blood on her lip, the robe pulling back over her legs.

Sands reached into his back pocket. He pulled out a handkerchief and dabbed at his face, and his eyes opened wide when he saw the bloodstains.

"You'll never find out now," he said. "Never! You hear me?"

She looked at him, trying to think of a way to reach him, wanting this news about Johnny, thinking, I've given you the most I could give.

"Hank . . ." she said, the anger out of her now, only the desire for the information remaining.

Sands laughed shrilly, a high laugh that fled to the ceiling of the room. He kept dabbing his torn flesh and laughing.

"Hank, is he hurt? Can you tell me that? Is Johnny hurt?"

"You dumb li'l whore," Sands said. "You think I'm goan tell you now? You can bust an' you can rot, but you never goan get it out o' me no more. No matter what you do now. You understan' that? You ain' gettin' nothin' from me!"

"Hank, I did what you said!"

"Shut up! Shut up an' listen to me. I got information, all right, I got mighty pow'ful information. But you ain' gettin' nothin'. You give to me, but you ain't gettin' nothin' in return. Not a damn thing."

He walked to the door, about to leave, and then a new idea seemed to strike him. He turned and said, "I'll tell you sutthin' else, Cindy Matthews. I hope that sonovabitch drops dead out there. I hope we has a blizzard tonight, an' I hope his goddamn arm falls off, an' I hope the mis'able bastard freezes hisself to death, thass what I hope."

He opened the door and then slammed it shut behind him, and Cindy lay on the linoleum covering the floor, and she listened to his laughter outside in the hallway. She wiped the blood from her lip, and then she kept listening to the laughter until it drifted down the staircase and faded.

Chapter Twelve

He felt weak all at once.

He'd felt fine up on the roof, and later just roaming the streets, trying to think of a lead to Luis' killer. But it was dark now, and there was a cold wind in the streets, and up ahead he could see the lights of the Savoy, and he could hear the muted beat of the music, and then the weakness came, suddenly.

It hit him in the legs first, a drained feeling, as if someone had suddenly stolen his bones. And then the lassitude spread to his groin, and then he knew he would really be sick because he always felt that weak draining in his groin when he was ill, even when he was a kid and had bronchitis.

He thought, I should have eaten more.

I should have seen a doctor.

The weakness spread, and the lights of the Savoy began to merge with the street lights and then the stars until the whole business pinwheeled around in his head. He didn't want to collapse, but he couldn't control his legs. He stumbled sideways, slamming against the fender of a new car. I can't pass out, he thought, I can't.

But the pinwheel spun into a crazy gray, and the gray turned black and then blacker, and he heard "The Two-O'Clock Jump" blasting from up there someplace, and then his shoulder hit the fender of the car, and he fell to the pavement and didn't hear the music any more.

Marcia Clarke had added the "e" to her name when she was nineteen. Until then, she'd been plain Marcia Clark, daughter of James Clark. The addition of the "e" was a way of declaring her independence, and also an attempt at sophistication. When Marcia added the "e," she also left the apartment of her parents on Pelham Parkway and found herself an apartment in Washington Heights. She was attending Brooklyn College at the time, and what with traveling time and asserting her new-found independence, Marcia was a very busy little girl.

For a little girl, Marcia was not at all unattractive. She had blonde hair and green eyes that were flecked with an inner circle of deep yellow. She owned a trim figure, with a narrow waist and a 34C bust, a bust she was inordinately proud of. She liked men to look at her bust. She also liked men to look at her legs, which were good legs, and she liked to remind men and women alike that "good things come in small packages."

Marcia was a model of deportment, except the time she'd worn a very low-cut gown to a senior tea, distracting most of the red-blooded Brooklyn College males, and driving some members of the faculty practically frantic. This, too—in Marcia's reasoning—was a way of showing her independence. When she was graduated from Brooklyn, she took a job as a laboratory technician. She still maintained her apartment in Washington Heights, but being denied senior teas Marcia was forced to find other means of asserting her independence.

Tonight she had danced with a total of twelve colored men. She was very proud of that fact. She had never been to the Savoy Ballroom before, and here, her first time, she'd danced with twelve colored men.

At first she'd been a little frightened. She was not nineteen any longer, nor was she twenty-one and attending a senior tea in a low-cut gown. And wearing a low-cut gown to a senior tea is not exactly the same thing as wearing a low-cut gown to the Savoy Ballroom.

And her gown *was* cut low. Apparently a lot of people had been looking. She'd danced with Mark only twice, and since then she hadn't been free once, and all the men she'd danced with were colored, and she was truly excited. It was like being in a foreign land. She couldn't understand a lot of the talk, and the local jokes passed over her head completely. The music was strange, too, a wild sort of music that spread to the bones. She'd have to do this more often, even if Mark didn't like it.

Mark definitely did not like it.

Mark had not liked the idea to begin with, but she had insisted.

He had a few fortifying shots before they drove into Harlem, and the fortifying shots had put him into a semistupor. In that stupor, he watched Marcia cavorting about with various men of various hues.

When the thirteenth man asked for her hand, Marcia smiled graciously and curtsied, bowing over low, the front of her dress billowing out over the 34C bust.

"You're number thirteen," she said, and Mark mumbled, and the tall Negro just smiled and whisked her onto the dance floor. She watched Mark from the circle of the Negro's arms.

"You like Harlem?" the Negro asked.

"Oh, yes," she said. She felt his arm tighten around her waist. She felt his cheek against hers, and she wondered if she should pull away, but she thought, Oh, the hell with it.

"This is only a small part of Harlem," the man said. "You should see all of it."

"Should I?" she asked coyly.

"I mean, if you're of a mind to."

"I hadn't thought of it."

"I mean, if your boy friend wouldn't mind."

"He's not my boy friend," she said, giggling. "He just escorted me here."

"Then mightn't we ditch him? I mean, if you—"

"I don't think so," Marcia said, but she did not take her cheek from the man's, nor did she move away from his tight embrace.

When he brought her back to Mark, he said, "I'll see

you a little later," and she smiled pertly. Mark was still sulking.

"Are you angry, little boy?" she asked.

"Nope," Mark said, his speech a little thick, the liquor still reeling around inside his brain. "You can go to hell with one of these jigs, for all I care."

"Mark! For heaven's sake!"

"What's the matter?" he asked, lifting one eyebrow.

"Watch the way you're talking," she whispered. "If one of them should hear—"

"Hell with 'm," he said grandly, using his arm in a musketeer gesture. "Le's get the hell out of here, Marcia, right now."

"I'm having fun," she said simply.

"Well, I'm not." Mark nodded emphatically, the gesture made bigger because he was still feeling the liquor. He lowered his voice intimately. "You should see the poisoned darts the girls're flingin' at you, baby. They don't like you one bit, not one little bit, nossir."

"Are they really?" Marcia asked, smiling and sucking in a dress-filling breath. She could not keep the smugness off her face.

"They are really," Mark affirmed. "They will probably rip off all your clothes soon, an' carry your head on a pike."

"Mark!"

"They will. An ol' tribal custom."

The thought of having all her clothes ripped from her was not unappealing. A sort of a white goddess. Stripped naked, with the tribesmen at her feet. She toyed with the idea, picturing it in her mind's eye.

"Well," she said, "I'm enjoying myself."

"O.K., Marcia, honey, sweetie, baby, doll, I'm leaving. You can stay here if you want to, but I'm leaving."

"Why don't you dance with some of the women?" Marcia asked.

Mark nodded sourly. "Change my luck? No, thanks. I'm goin' home. You comin' along, or do you want to stay? You pays your money and you takes your cherce."

"I'd really like to stay a little longer. The music is so—"

"So stay. I'll be seein' you, Marcia doll. Lessee now, wha's your number again?"

"Oh, Mark, you're being plain stupid."

"Agreed. 'Night, Marcia."

"Wait."

He whirled unsteadily. "Uhm?"

Marcia was angry. It showed in the flash of her eyes and the heave of her breasts. "What are you, a coward or something?" she asked.

"Me?" Mark considered this. "Yes," he said gravely. "I am a coward or something. 'Night."

"Wait," she said, "for God's sake, wait." She paused to catch her breath, looking very pretty when she was angry, and knowing she looked very pretty. "I'll be very angry if you force me to leave."

"Nobody's forcin' you. Stay. Stay, honey. I don't care. I'm goin'."

"I'll go with you," she said suddenly, a little frightened at the thought of being left alone in Harlem. "But this is the last you'll see of me, Mark."

Mark shrugged. "O.K., if tha's what you want." He paused. "I'll get our coats."

They went out onto the sidewalk, and she did not take his arm. He walked crookedly, and she said coldly, "You're drunk, do you know that?"

"So I'm drunk. I must've been drunk to take you here in the first place."

"Oh, shut up."

"You sore at me?" he asked.

"Yes."

"Well, I don't care. Whattya think of that? I don' give a damn."

"I wonder how you'll feel in the morning, when you start remembering."

"I'll feel fine. Whattya think, you own me or something? We date a few times, an' right away—"

"A *few* times?"

"Yas, a few times," Mark shouted. He lowered his voice. "All right, a few months, all right? Still, I don't have to go chasin' to Harlem to see you dancin' with a lot of jigs."

"Stop calling them that!"

"It's what they are, isn't it?"

"You're making me sick," Marcia said. "You'd better shut up."

"I didn't know you were so in love with—"

"It's not that. It's just that I can see nothing wrong with frequenting a Negro dance estab—"

"Oh, here comes your Public Speaking Two voice. Three-minute speech. Watch your 'nunciation, now. You're being timed. Go!"

"Oh, go to hell," Marcia said.

They walked in silence for a block, and then he said, "Here's the goddamn car."

"Look," she said. "On the sidewalk."

"Huh?" Mark glanced down to where the figure huddled against his right front wheel. "Oh, f'r crissakes, tha's all I need."

"He's hurt," Marcia said, her hand to her mouth.

"Hurt, my ass. He's drunk. Come on, give me a hand here."

"Mark, he's hurt. We've got to help him."

Mark stooped down and lifted the man's hand out of the gutter. "There," he said. "Now I won't run over him. Come on, Marcia, get in."

"He's sick, Mark, I know he's sick. Can't you see that? My God, can't you see that?"

"I can see he's drunk," Mark said doggedly. "What the hell do you think I am, Alcoholics Anonymous?"

Marcia stooped down and opened the tweed coat. She felt for the man's heart. "He's sick," she said. "Let's take him to a doctor."

"You're out of your mind."

"Help me get him in the car."

"*My* car?"

127

"Yes, your car. Mark, if you don't help me now, I'll never—"

"Use your head, Marcia," he pleaded. "The guy's drunk."

"Can you smell any whisky on him?"

"Well . . ."

"Unlock the car."

Mark squeezed his eyes shut. "Marcia, you are the craziest . . ."

"Unlock the car."

"All right. All right, goddamnit, but this ties it. This really ties it. This is it, baby. You can just—"

"Hurry up."

He unlocked the door of the new Oldsmobile, and then lifted the man onto the front seat. Marcia squeezed in beside him, and then Mark went around to the door near the driver's seat and opened it.

"Are you sober enough to drive?" she asked.

"I'm sober, all right," Mark said coldly.

The figure between them stirred.

Mark turned the ignition key and looked at the man. "He's coming around."

"We've got to get him to a doctor," Marcia said.

"I don't understand why you think he's—"

"Because I know he's not drunk, and people who are well don't go lying in the gutter."

"He wasn't lying in the gutter. He was—"

"Let's take him to a doctor," Marcia said firmly, "and let's hurry."

"No," the man said.

He spoke so suddenly that he startled Marcia.

"There," Mark said, "I told you."

"Sssssh!" she said sharply.

"No," the man said again. "No doctor. Please. My arm'll be all right."

He spoke so softly that she almost didn't hear him.

"His *what*?" Mark asked.

"His arm! You see, he *is* hurt. Now will you listen? Find a doctor."

"No," the man said, shaking his head this time. "No, please. No doctor. Please, no doctor."

"He doesn't want to go to a doctor," Mark said.

"I don't care what he wants. We'll take him to one."

"No doctor," the man mumbled. "Please, please."

"He doesn't want one," Mark said firmly. "Look, Marcia, let's play this smart, shall we? He's coming around now. Let's leave him outside and forget about it. Let's get out of Harlem."

"No," Marcia said. "We'll take him home. We can at least do that." She shook the figure beside her. "Can you tell us where you live?" she asked. She could see the man was sick.

The man shook his head. "Don't take me home," he said.

"Now, what the hell!" Mark said.

"Maybe he was in a street fight," Marcia said. "Maybe they're still waiting for him. There are always street fights in Harlem."

"Well, what the hell are we supposed to do? He doesn't want a doctor and he doesn't want to go home. Are we supposed to hold his hand all night?"

Marcia considered for a moment, biting her lip. "We'll go to my place," she said suddenly.

"What!"

"You heard me. We'll take him to my place."

"Now I know you're nuts. Now I know it. If I wasn't sure before, I know it now. You're going to take a strange drunk—"

"He's not drunk. You heard him mention his arm."

"All right, so you're taking a street brawler into your home. The place to take him is the police."

"Don't be absurd."

"Suppose he's . . . done something? Marcia, what the hell do you know about him? Just a bum lying in the gutter."

"He wasn't lying in the gutter," Marcia said. "You said so yourself."

"All right," Mark said, throwing up his hands. "All right, sister, it's your house. You can start giving out free soup on Christmas Day, for all I care." He moved the car out into the street. "I'm washing my hands of it. It's your headache."

"It's my headache," she repeated. She felt the man stir on the seat beside her. She put her arm on the seat behind him, and he fell over, his head resting on her breast. She felt a strange mixture of motherly protectiveness and womanly interest. She inhaled a deep breath, feeling the pressure of his head on her breast. A smile formed on her mouth. Beside her, Mark drove grimly, saying nothing.

He put the man down on the couch, and then he stood over him, looking down at him.

"There," he said.

Marcia took off her coat and threw it over the back of a chair.

"Thank you, Mark," she said. "It was nice of you to help me get him upstairs."

"It's your funeral," he said.

"Well, thanks anyway."

"You sure you don't want to change your mind?"

"About what?"

"About him. If he *is* hurt, then we should call the police."

"No. The police aren't going to help him, can't you see that? If he was hurt in a street fight, the police will only lock him up. Mark, he needs understanding, not imprisonment."

"How do you know he was hurt in a street fight?"

"I don't. I'll ask him when he comes around."

Mark stood uncertainly. "Marcia . . ."

"You can go if you like," she said.

"I'll stay, if you want me to."

"I still haven't forgotten everything that happened, Mark."

"Well, I'll be damned if I'm going to leave you here with a jig who may turn out to be a rape artist!"

"I don't like your language and I don't like the things

you're thinking. I think you'd better go air out your mind."

"Public Speaking Two again," he said.

"And I don't particularly relish your cracks about my college education. If you feel that way about it—"

"Marcia, let me stay."

"I think you'd better go. I've had quite enough of you for one evening."

"All right," he said. "All right. All right, I'll go. I hope he *does* . . ."

Marcia smiled triumphantly. "He very well *might*," she said, knowing she was hurting Mark and wanting to hurt him now. Mark went to the door, hesitated.

"I'll call you tomorrow."

"Don't bother," she answered coldly.

He hesitated another moment, looked at the man on the couch again, and then left. She watched the door close behind him, and then she got up to lock it. She was very glad he'd left. There was a strange excitement within her, an excitement she did not quite understand. She felt extremely tolerant. Yes, tolerant; that was the only word she could think of to describe this feeling of brotherhood within her. At the same time, she felt as if she were doing something completely dangerous and reckless. She did, after all, know nothing at all about the man on her couch. Except that he was attractive in a slender, supple way, and of course that didn't enter into it at all. What she'd said to Mark, that was just to annoy him. She wouldn't even consider . . .

The man stirred, and she went to him quickly. He blinked his eyes open and then sat bolt upright, looking around the room. He seemed poised to run, so she put her hand on his arm and said, "It's all right."

"Where am I?" he said quickly.

"In my apartment."

He blinked and then looked her fully in the face. "Who are you?"

"Marcia Clarke." She smiled pleasantly. "Who are you?"

"Johnny," he said. "Johnny L—" He caught himself. "Johnny."

"How's your arm, Johnny?"

He glanced unconsciously at his right arm. "It's all right," he said quickly. He wet his lips and looked around the apartment again.

"Take off your coat, why don't you?"

"Well, thanks, but I got to be—"

"Go ahead, please. Make yourself comfortable." Marcia smiled archly. "I'm not going to bite you, Johnny."

"Well, maybe for a minute," he said. He shrugged out of his coat, and Marcia took it from him and carried it into the bedroom. She put the coat down on the bed, and when she returned to the living room she said, "Were you in a street fight?"

"No. No, not exactly."

They looked at each other awkwardly for a few moments.

"Is your arm hurt badly?" she asked.

"It got cut," he said. "It'll be all right."

"Oh."

"Where'd you find me?" he asked.

"Outside the Savoy Ballroom."

"You were at the Savoy?"

"Yes." Marcia paused. "Is there anything wrong with that?"

"No, nothing," he said.

"Or do you think the white man should stay in his place?" Marcia smiled, enjoying her own little joke.

"I . . . There's nothing wrong with going to the Savoy," he said.

"But you don't think I should have gone there?"

"Miss, it's a free country. You can go wherever you like."

"But not Harlem."

"I didn't say that." He bit his lip. "Look, I think I better cut out. Can I have my coat, please?"

"Oh, stay put. You've had a shock. You need some rest."

"Yeah, I guess so."

Marcia sat next to him on the couch. "How'd you get cut, Johnny?"

"What difference does it make?"

"I want to know." She felt extremely courageous, sitting next to a man who'd been cut, especially a Negro. To show how courageous she felt, she leaned over, and the dress fell away from her breasts. She saw his eyes on her, and she smiled.

"I just got cut, that's all," he said.

"Did a woman cut you?"

"A woman? No, no. What gave you that idea?"

"I heard colored women are very jealous of their men."

"Oh." He paused awkwardly. "No, a woman didn't cut me."

"Who did?"

"A man."

"Why?"

"He felt like cutting me, I guess. Look . . ."

"What did he cut you with? A razor?"

"No," he said a little harshly. "Look, miss . . ."

"A knife?"

"He cut me with the broken end of a syringe. He was a dope fiend, and I broke his syringe by accident, and he stabbed me with it. That's what he cut me with."

"You're kidding," she said.

"All right, I'm kidding. Now can I have my coat?"

"Rest a while," she said, not knowing why she wanted him to stay, but still feeling this strange mixture of tolerance and excitement. "Are there a lot of addicts in Harlem?"

"I suppose," he said wearily.

"Are you an addict?"

"Hell, no."

"I was only asking."

"Well, I'm not one."

"You've never touched the stuff?"

"A little tea, and once or twice a sniff of C."

"A little what?"

"Marijuana. There's no harm in marijuana. It's just the bait, you see, to get you hooked on the bigger junk. Not everybody in Harlem's an addict."

"I know, but it's terrible the way these men are allowed to sell their drugs."

"They ain't allowed," he said. "The cops are always after them."

"But they still sell it."

"Sure."

"Why didn't you want us to take you to a doctor?"

"Because . . ." He paused and studied her face. "Did I say that?"

"Yes."

"I guess maybe because the cut is nothing to worry about."

"Why didn't you want us to take you home?"

"I . . . I just didn't want you to."

"Are you in some trouble?"

"No."

"You are, aren't you?"

"No," he insisted.

"Then why didn't you want us to take you home?"

"My stepfather beats me," he lied.

"Does he really?"

"Yes, with a razor strop. Every night. Before going to bed. He can't sleep well unless he beats me."

"You poor thing," she said. She looked into his eyes and asked, "Would you like a drink or something? A drink is supposed to be good for shock."

"All right," he said.

"Scotch, rye, bourbon?"

"Anything. I don't care."

She leaned over to rise, and she felt his eyes on the front of her dress again. A tremor of excitement worked its way up her spine. She smiled and walked across the room to the bar, lifting a bottle of bourbon and pouring rapidly. She filled another glass for herself, and then brought both glasses to the free-form cocktail table in front of the couch.

"Cheers," she said. She lifted her glass to her lips,

peering over the brim, still feeling very dangerous, and beginning to feel a little like a *femme fatale*.

"Drink hearty," he said.

He drained his glass, and she sipped at hers and then put it down on the table.

"Make yourself comfortable," she said. "I want to change."

He looked at her curiously for a moment, and she smiled and then walked to the bedroom. She closed the door just a little ways, and then pulled her dress over her head. She did not know why she was doing all this, except that she felt very dangerous and very tolerant, and the mixture had made her a little heady. Besides, he seemed like such a cold fish, and he *was* attractive, really, and then again he was a Negro, and there was something about the entire thing that was very exciting. She took off her slip and folded it on the bed, alongside his overcoat. She touched the tweed of the coat, and then walked to the closet. She unclasped her bra and stepped out of her panties, and then she reached into the closet for something sheer, and then changed her mind abruptly.

There was such a thing as going too far, and she suddenly began questioning her own motives. Just what was she planning? Not that, certainly. Certainly not that. Let's get a hold on ourself, Marcia, she thought. She walked to the dresser and took out a skirt and sweater. She did not bother putting the underwear on again. She pulled the sweater over the skirt, then smoothed the skirt over her hips and tightened her breasts inside the sweater, thinking they looked better without a bra, and they certainly felt a lot better. She took one last look in the mirror, and then opened the door and stepped into the living room. He was still sitting on the couch. His head was in his hands. She cleared her throat, and he lifted his head. She started walking across the room, knowing her breasts were bobbing, and knowing his eyes were focused on them, but not caring.

"Don't you feel well?" she asked soothingly.

"I feel fine. I was trying to figure why I passed out."

"Well, don't worry about it. You're safe now."

"Am I?" he asked, and she thought she detected a curiously sardonic note in his voice.

"Of course you are. Would you like another drink?"

"No."

He sat quietly for a moment or two. She pulled her legs up under her on the couch, and then she tucked her skirt around them demurely, making a big production of it, exaggerating the simple maneuver until it couldn't fail to attract his attention. And even while she was doing this, she told herself, Marcia, don't be absurd. Marcia, don't play with fire. You don't even know who he is.

"What are you thinking?" she asked.

"Nothing."

"Come on, what are you thinking?"

"I was just wondering where I'm going to spend the night."

"Oh." She felt the excitement flare within her, and somehow, beneath the excitement, a tiny flame of fear began licking at her mind. "I . . . I see," she said. She tucked her skirt more firmly beneath her, as if his sentence had suddenly changed the entire scheme of things. It was one thing to . . . well, to be in control of the situation, but it was another to have the situation forced upon you. She did not like any situation forced upon her. A forced situation was an intrusion on her independence. Besides, she really didn't know who or what he was, and that brought to mind another question.

"Why do you need a place to spend the night?"

"My father beats me," he said sarcastically.

"No, really. Why can't you go home?"

"I can't, that's all."

"Does it have anything to do with your cut?"

"Yes, yes, that's it," he said. "My father can't stand the sight of blood."

"You're not telling me the truth."

"I know I'm not."

"Don't you think you owe me the truth?"

"No," he said. "I don't owe you anything. No one asked you to bring me here."

He spoke so bitterly, so angrily, that she was suddenly really afraid. She wanted to ask her next question, but she didn't want to hear the answer. She was painfully aware of her naked bosom beneath the taut wool of the sweater. She glanced downward self-consciously, seeing the sharp points thrusting against the wool. She grew panicky all at once, and she lifted her arm to cover her breasts, thankful that he was not watching her. She remembered all the stories she'd heard about Negro men and white women, and she tried to tell herself the stories were all foolish, but she couldn't drive out the fear, and she kept thinking of what Mark had said before he'd left. She was more frightened because she'd brought all this on herself, taking a strange black man into her home, a man who could be anything, a murderer, a gangster, a rapist. She could feel the perspiration starting on her brow.

She wet her lips, wondering if she should leave the room to put on a robe or something. But if she walked across the room, his eyes would be on her all the way, watching her flesh against the tightness of her skirt. She wet her lips again. She did not feel very tolerant any more. She felt frightened, plain frightened. This man beside her, who was he? What was he running from? Why didn't he want to be taken to a doctor?

"Are . . ." She wet her lips and swallowed the solid lump in her throat. "Are the police after you?"

"No," he said quickly.

She could not let it drop. She had her answer, but it was not the answer she wanted. And just as she had deliberately fed her own excitement earlier, she now fed her fear, deriving a crackling, spitting sort of pleasure from it.

"You *are* running from the police," she insisted.

"No," he said again.

"Tell me the truth," she said.

He looked at her face, and she hoped the fear was not

showing there. "All right," he said, "I'm running from the police."

"Wh . . . what did you do?"

"Nothing."

"If the police are after you, you must have done something."

"I didn't do anything, believe me. They say I killed a man, but—"

"Killed a man!"

"But I didn't do it, believe me. Look, miss . . ."

"I . . . I need another drink," she said. She rose and walked shakily to the bar, trying to keep the swing out of her hips. He had killed a man, but no, he said he hadn't killed a man, and yet the police were after him. She poured a jigger full of bourbon, and then threw it down hastily, her hand trembling.

She put down her glass and made a stroking motion at her throat, her arm covering the front of her sweater. She could feel the fear mounting inside her, and there was nothing enjoyable about it now. She kept cursing herself for having been such a fool. My God, what could have been on her mind to have pulled such a crazy stunt? A man wanted for murder. Oh, my God, Mark, where are you? Come back, Mark, please. Take this . . . this black murderer away.

He sat on the couch, staring at the floor. He looked up suddenly with a smile on his face.

"Are you afraid of me now?" he asked.

"No," she said quickly. "Don't . . . don't be silly."

"You've nothing to be afraid of."

"I . . . know."

He kept staring at her with the curious smile on his face, and she wondered what he was thinking and suddenly she seemed to know just what he was thinking, and she expected him to get off the couch any minute and come across the room to her. She stood by the bar, petrified, waiting for the move. When it did not come, she cleared her throat and said, "I'm . . . a little chilly. I think I'll put on a robe."

She went into the bedroom, closing the door behind

138

her, not noticing in her haste that it was still partially open. She ran past the tweed coat and the slip on her bed, and then she stepped over her panties and bra where they lay on the floor in a heap. She went directly to the phone, lifting the receiver quickly.

She waited for a dial tone, and then she dialed the "O" for Operator.

When the voice came on the line, she said, "Get me the police. Quickly, please."

She waited, hearing the phone ring on the other end. She heard the outer door of her apartment slam just as the voice on the line said, "Sergeant Haggerty."

She paused, listening.

"Never . . . never mind," she said. She hung up quickly, and then walked into the living room, hoping she'd been right. She sighed heavily.

The Negro was gone.

She called Mark immediately, and when he got there, about ten minutes later, she sobbingly told him the whole story, leaving out the emotions she had felt, but telling him everything else. Then, after she had quieted down, Mark took the tweed coat out to the incinerator in the hallway, and opened the metal door and shoved it down the chute.

Chapter Thirteen

She was standing before the full-length mirror in her dressing room, having just come off the floor. She stood in her sequined bra and G string, wearing only those and high-heeled slippers. She stood and looked at her body, thinking of what Hank Sands had done to that body, and wanting to crawl out of her skin, leave it somewhere the way a snake does. She wanted to dress quickly. She wanted to cover her body, hide it. She had felt a peculiar revulsion tonight on the floor. Hank Sands had not been in the crowd, but she could feel his eyes in the eyes of every man in the club. It was not a wholesome feeling. For the first time since she'd been working at the Yahoo, she'd felt ashamed of her job.

She turned from the mirror, reaching for the underwear piled over a chair. She was taking off one slipper when the knock sounded on the door.

"Who is it?" she said.

"Police," the voice answered.

"Just a moment." She took a silk robe from a hanger on the screen and pulled it on quickly, belting it tightly around her waist. She tightened the strap on her slipper again, and went to the door.

"Yes?" she said coldly.

"May I come in?" the man said.

"All right," she answered.

She held the door wide, and he entered the small room. He did not look like a cop. He was thin, and his hair was going, and he owned a nose that should have belonged to a hawk. He looked around the room, seemingly embarrassed.

"What do you want?" she asked. She folded her arms

across the front of her robe and leaned back against the dressing table.

He reached into his pocket and flipped open a wallet. She saw the shield and nodded, and he said, "My name is Dave Trachetti. Detective Second/Grade."

"So?" she said. She reached over for a package of cigarettes, shaking one loose and hanging it on her lip. She thought he might offer to light it. When he didn't, she struck a match herself, shook it out, and dropped it to the floor.

Trachetti smiled, still looking a little embarrassed. "I saw your show, Miss Matthews. It was very nice. I was out front when—"

"I don't go out with white men," Cindy said. "Not even if they're cops."

"That's not it, Miss Matthews. I wanted to talk to you about Johnny Lane."

Cindy stopped the hand with the cigarette an inch away from her mouth.

"Oh," she said. "So that's it. I'm sorry I misunderstood. So many men come back here wanting . . ."

"I understand," Trachetti said. He wet his lips nervously. "It must be a . . . trying profession."

Cindy did not smile. "But about Johnny, I don't know anything. We split up a long while ago. I told you that before."

"You don't know where he is?" Trachetti asked.

"No, I don't. Why don't you go find him yourself? Do me a favor, and find him yourself. Leave me alone."

"I wish I *could* find him," Trachetti said.

"So you can pin a phony rap on him?"

"That's just it, Miss Matthews. We . . ."

"Johnny didn't kill the spic, but that doesn't matter to you. You've got yourself a sucker, so now everything will be clear with the commissioner. As long as your nose is clean, what do you care? Get out, why don't you? You're wasting your time, and I'm getting chilly, and I want to dress. Get the hell out, unless you're going to book me for something."

"I should have been a bus driver," Trachetti said. "I swear to God I should have been a bus driver. Look, Miss Matthews, I came here to tell you we caught Luis Ortega's killer."

She stared at him, and then she blinked her eyes, and then she leaned back against the dressing table again, almost as if she'd dropped there involuntarily.

"You . . . you . . ."

"Not Johnny Lane. Another guy. We've got a confession. That's what I came here to tell you. I thought you might like to know. I thought you'd want to tell Johnny—if you can find him again after being split up so long." He couldn't resist the sarcasm.

"You . . . you don't want him any more?"

"He's clean," Trachetti said. "I told you, we've got a confession."

"Then he's running for nothing! He doesn't have to run. You say someone else did it?"

"Didn't you know that all along, Miss Matthews?"

"Yes, but I mean . . . Oh, God, his arm. His arm is cut. I've got to find him. I've got to tell him."

"Yes," Trachetti said.

He watched her go to the closet and take a coat from its hanger. She pulled the coat on over her robe, and the silk pulled back to show the naked length of her leg and thigh and the sequined sparkle of the G string. She belted the coat quickly and started for the door.

"It's pretty cold out there," Trachetti said. "Maybe you ought to . . ."

She stopped just inside the doorway. She turned and said, "Thank you. I'm sorry I was . . . Thank you. Thank you very much."

"Do you think you can find him?" he asked.

Cindy hesitated for a moment. "I hope so," she said. "Oh, God, I hope so."

It was very cold, and Johnny Lane was very tired of running.

He thought of the tweed coat he'd left back in Washington Heights, and he thought, Barney is going to be sore as hell. He wondered if he shouldn't have stayed up in the Heights someplace, but with that crazy chick on the phone yelling to the cops, he was better off in Harlem. He still couldn't figure her out. What the hell was her game anyway? He'd met up with nuts before, but she took the prize.

The cold was biting, and he walked quickly, trying to work up some heat in his body. Goddamnit, why had he let her take the coat in the first place? Hadn't he learned his lesson with coats yet? How many coats and jackets and assorted wearing apparel do you have to lose before catching on? Why couldn't the day have stayed the way it was this afternoon? He hadn't needed a coat then. He'd had a coat when he didn't need it. And now, when it was colder than hell, he was running around in his shirt sleeves.

He walked up 125th Street, watching the people bundled in their overcoats, watching them and wondering where they were all going. It was very late at night. Were they going home to clean sheets and a warm bed? What did a warm bed feel like? When's the last time I slept in a warm bed? he wondered. I slept in a warm bed at Cindy's place. What's Cindy thinking by now? Just a penciled note, and I haven't even called her or anything. But how did I know I was going to pass out, and how did I know that dizzy broad was going to drag me up to her place? I should have played it cool. I should have given it to her the way she wanted it, told her yes, I'd been in a street fight, yes, I was a poor neglected nigger, yes, I needed her help and her comfort. I should have played it the cool way, instead of scaring her out of her wits. What the hell did I tell her the truth for?

And now Barney's coat is up there, and man, he's going to be sore as hell. Suppose I told Barney the truth? He'd still be sore as hell, and I can't blame him much, it was a nice coat. And he stuck his neck out for me, he did do that, even if he didn't want to. And those other guys, The Flower and the other guy, they didn't

143

have to get me that boat. They got it for me after I told them the truth.

Or maybe they thought I was lying, and besides, they just helped me to get even with the bulls. They didn't give a damn about truth or lies or whatever. But they did get me the boat. I wonder if I should go back to the boat tonight.

How can I spend another night on that tub, with those goddamn rats roaming around? Without even a coat this time, with all that cold, damp wind blowing off the water, and the stink of garbage, but most of all the rats crawling around. Even if I didn't see a single rat, I could feel them out there. No, I wouldn't go back to that boat if you gave me a million dollars. I'd freeze to death there, and I'm gonna freeze to death here, too, unless I get a place to stay and damned soon. Why does it get so tough once night rolls around? Because then you're noticeable on the streets, jerk. Then a roaming Snow White will spot you, and then it's the kiss-off. Lord, I'm cold, I've never been so damn cold in all my life.

He passed the darkened windows of the shops on 125th Street, heading west, wondering just where he was going. He wondered, too, what the cops were doing now.

He could almost see them bustling around downtown, getting out a general alarm or whatever they got out. Would they use bloodhounds? Did city cops ever use bloodhounds? All he needed was a pack of mutts chasing him up Lenox Avenue. He smiled, the picture striking him somehow as amusing. He could just see his photo on page four of the Daily News, Johnny Lane up a lamppost, his pants seat torn to shreds, while the mutts stood up on their hind legs and barked and snapped. Caption: "Killer at Bay."

Bay, you know. The hounds baying, you know.

Very funny, he told himself, but you can't wrap a joke around your back, and a laugh won't stop the wind, and the wind was sure cold.

So what now? First, he needed a place for the night.

Now there's a simple thing. How about the Waldorf, Lane? All right, how about the Waldorf? No, I don't think so. Really, my dear, after all, the *Wal*-dorf? Hardly. Not for Johnny Lane. Nothing but the best for Johnny Lane.

Well, how about Cindy's pad, then? That's the place to be. That's the place, but the cops don't want me to be there, so we'll just stay away from there, too, thank you.

A hotel, then. Any hotel. A hotel in Brooklyn or Staten Island or any goddamn place. Sure, why not? Except what makes you think the hotels aren't as alerted tonight as they were last night? And how do you check into a hotel with no luggage and in your shirt sleeves? Damnit, it's getting colder by the minute.

So where? Where?

He began giving the problem serious thought, because he recognized freezing as a very serious thing. He did not want to pass out again. He might not be so lucky next time, even if the broad had turned out to be a little loony. So in his mind he turned over every nook and cranny in Harlem, examining it minutely. When he got the idea, he considered it gravely, and then he inspected it, and then he tested it again for size.

There was a warehouse off 125th down near Lex, was it? Or was it 126th, or where was it exactly? He'd find it, that was for sure. A warehouse where one of the furniture stores kept all its new goods. There was a window the guys used to sneak in through, where one of the bars was loose and capable of being swung out of position. They'd taken Carmen Diaz there once when they were just kids, and they'd had a jolly old time on the mats the movers used to wrap around the furniture. He wouldn't forget that time so easily because Carmen had really known the score, and even if the other guys were yelling for him to hurry up it had still been damned fine. Nor would he forget how they had got into the warehouse, because that had been the trickiest part, and he could remember seeing Carmen's backside under her skirt as she squeezed through

145

the bars. There was no watchman because all the windows were barred, and who the hell would want to steal furniture, anyway? (He forgot that Mikie the Turk, for one, had wanted to steal furniture, and that he'd lugged an end table all the way downstairs, only to discover he couldn't get it through the narrow opening the loose bar presented.) One of the guys had lived down there, near the Triboro, on the colored fringe bordering Wop Harlem. They'd kidded with the guy about not being high-class enough to move into what was *really* Harlem. They'd kidded him until the guy came up with the little spic whore, and then they didn't kid him any more.

He reversed his course abruptly, heading east. It was probably best, anyway, to stay out of the Harlem he knew well. In fact, what was he doing on a main drag like 125th? He cut down to 124th, and then turned left on Third Avenue, noting the mixture of whites and blacks and spics. He kept walking uptown, and he spotted the warehouse when he looked up one of the side streets. The street was very dark, and that was just the way he wanted it. He saw a cat cross the street, and then run when she spotted him. There wasn't a human being in sight. He walked to the fence surrounding the warehouse and climbed over it rapidly, dropping to all fours on the other side. The yard was empty and silent. He looked around for a few moments, probing his memory, getting his bearings, and then he went directly to the window with the loose bar.

Suppose they fixed the bar? he thought suddenly. It was a long time ago. Suppose . . .

He began trying the bars, losing hope almost before he started. And then suddenly the fifth bar came free under his hands. He moved it to one side, and then worked open the window, expecting an alarm to go off. He waited, listening. There was no alarm. Quickly he squeezed through the window. It was a tighter fit than it had been when he was a kid, but he got through and dropped to the concrete floor, reaching up to close the window behind him.

There was the smell of dust all around him, and a silence like being underwater at the beach. Like suddenly ducking your head under the water, cutting off the locust hum of people that hangs over the sand and the air, hearing only the cool vastness of the ocean. The furniture was stacked all over the place, covered with mats and sheets. The windows were dirty, and he could barely make out the headlamps of passing cars through them.

It was warm. He was thankful for that. It was warm, and maybe there were rats in furniture warehouses, too, but he doubted it. Why would a rat go where there was no food? Besides, he could pull one of the heavy mats over his body and head, and then he wouldn't have anything to worry about, even if there were rats.

He was looking forward to a good night's sleep. In the morning he would . . . In the morning. There was always the goddamn morning.

He found the old iron stairs, and he began climbing to the third floor, where the mats had been stacked that time with Carmen. He could remember the incident as clearly as if it were happening now, the gang of them stealing up these same iron steps, Mikie shushing everybody, and Carmen's skirt flashing around her mature legs. There had been a high, excited flush on her face, and she had giggled all the way upstairs. He climbed steadily, lost in the memory. When he heard the sudden voice, he turned and was ready to run, but he'd already been spotted and he didn't want a bullet in the back now.

"Hold it, Mac," the voice said.

A watchman, he thought.

He froze solid because there was no sense running now. Maybe he could bull it through, and if not, he still had a good left arm, and he still knew how to throw a fist. He waited in the darkness, hearing the footsteps ring closer on the iron stairs. The man came up to him, a big man barely visible in the dimness.

"Whattaya want, Mac?" the man asked.

A white man, Johnny thought, a white man. This makes it even better. This makes it just grand.

"You the watchman?" he asked.

The big man laughed. "Watchman, huh? A watchman? You on the bum, too, kid?"

He felt immensely relieved all at once, so relieved that he almost smiled. "Yeah," he said, "I'm on the bum."

"Come on up," the man said. "You want a cup of java?"

"Man, I could use some," he said.

The big man laughed again and reached out for Johnny's arm. He tried to pull away, but he wasn't quick enough, and he winced in pain, and when the strangled cry came from his throat, the big man looked at him curiously.

"You hurt, huh, kid?" he asked. There was no sympathy in his voice. There was, instead, a crafty sound, as if the man had made a very valuable discovery and was putting it away in a deep, black satchel.

"Come on," he said, his voice oily now. "We'll get you that java."

They started up the steps together, the man walking several paces behind Johnny. When they reached the third floor, he took Johnny's elbow and said, "This way, kid."

Johnny peered into the darkness. He could see a glow in one corner of the room, and he could make out the muted hum of voices coming from that corner. The heavy mats were stacked all around the room, and he glanced at these briefly and then turned his attention back to the big man. The man led him to the circle of men huddled in the corner of the huge, concrete-floored room. An electric grill was plugged into an outlet, and a battered coffeepot rested on the glowing orange coils. Johnny looked at the circle of bearded faces, four men all told, four white men, five counting the big man who'd led him to the group. The men were smiling, but there was no mirth on their faces.

"Who you brung for dinner, Bugs?" one of the men asked.

"A nice young coon," the big man answered. "Hurt his poor little arm, though, didn't you, sonny?"

The eyes of the men fled to the bulkiness of the bandage under the shirt. He tried to move his right arm, but the eyes followed the movement and calculated the size of the bandage, and then shifted to his face, the mouths still smiling, but the smile never reaching those calculating eyes.

"Didn't you, punk?" Bugs asked. "Didn't you hurt your arm?"

Johnny wet his lips. "Yeah, I . . . I got cut." He didn't like the sound of the conversation, and he knew what "punk" meant in prison jargon, because he knew enough guys who'd been in and out of Riker's Island.

"Well, now, that's too bad, punk," one of the men in the circle said. "Now, that's too bad you got a cut on your arm."

"Maybe we got a nurse here can fix it up," another man said.

"Sure, we got a lot of nurses here, kid. We'll fix you up fine, kid. Hey, how about a cup of coffee for the coon?"

He wasn't sure now. He wasn't sure what they meant, and he wasn't sure whether they intended him harm or whether they were giving him sanctuary. He knew only that there were five of them, all white, and that he had only one good arm.

One of the men put a spoon into the pot and began stirring the coffee. Johnny watched him, saying nothing.

"How'd you hit on this place, punk?" Bugs asked.

"I just knew it, that's all."

"Oh? You from the neighborhood?"

"Harlem," Johnny said.

"Oh? A little far east, ain't you?"

"I guess," Johnny said.

"Well, don't you worry, kid. You come to the right place, didn't he, fellers?"

"He come to the right place, all right," one of the men in the circle said.

"You're just what we been needin'," another man put in.

Bugs chuckled. "Yessir, it was real lucky, your coming here. You don't know how lucky you are."

One of the men poured the coffee into a tin cup, and the strong aroma reached Johnny's nostrils, clung there. He wanted that coffee very badly, he wanted it almost desperately. There was an empty hole in his stomach, and he thought again of how little he'd eaten since he began running, and the hole seemed to enlarge itself. The man handed the cup to Bugs, and the steam rose in the orange glow of the grill, curling up around his smiling face.

"Harry makes a good cup of coffee," Bugs said. "Harry should have been somebody's wife, eh, Harry?" Bugs winked at the other men, and Johnny's eyes watched the circle. He spotted Harry then, a skinny guy with hardly any beard, a skinny guy with frightened eyes and a narrow mouth. Harry winced when Bugs spoke, and then he shrank farther back out of the circle.

"No more now," he said pleadingly, "huh Bugs? No more now?" He looked hopefully to Johnny, and Johnny felt the panic rise in him again, and he counted the men once more. Five of them. That hadn't changed. Not one bit, it hadn't.

"You can still make our coffee, can't you, Harry?" Bugs asked tenderly. "Now you can still do that for us, can't you, boy?"

"Sure," Harry said, almost eagerly, smiling. "Sure, Bugs. You know that."

"Makes a good cup of coffee," Bugs said, facing Johnny squarely now. "You want the coffee, punk?"

"I'd like a cup," Johnny said warily.

"Well," Bugs said, "he'd like a cup, fellers."

"Go on, Bugs, give it to him."

"Oh, now, wait a minute, just wait a minute. I mean,

150

coffee is coffee, now ain't it? You got the money to pay for this, punk?"

Maybe that was it. Maybe all they wanted was money.

"No," Johnny lied. "I'm broke."

"Well, now, ain't that a shame?" Bugs said, winking again at the other men.

"That's a real shame," one of the men in the circle said.

"My heart bleeds for the punk."

They sat around the orange coils, grinning like demons, leaning forward eagerly now, enjoying the way Bugs was handling this.

"How you 'spect to get any coffee unless you pay for it?" Bugs asked. "Coffee don't grow on trees, now."

"I guess not," Johnny said slowly. "Forget the coffee. I'll do without it."

"Aw, you hurt the punk's feelings, Bugs," one of the men said.

"Well, I didn't mean to do that. I sure didn't mean to do that."

"But you did, Bugs. Look at how he's sulkin' there."

"Now, now," Bugs said, "no need to take that attitude, is there, boys? We'll let you have the coffee, won't we, boys?"

"Sure, Bugs," one of the men said. "Hell, the punk don't need no money."

"That money you use up in Harlem prolly wouldn't be no good here, anyway."

"Why, sure," Bugs said. "Naw, you don't need no money, punk. We willing to barter. You know how to horse-trade, punk?"

"I don't want the coffee," Johnny said firmly. He was already figuring how he'd make his break, because he knew a break was in the cards, and the way the cards were falling, he'd have to make the break soon. The orange glow of the grill was the only light in the room, that and the feeble moonlight that came through the window. He calculated this, and he watched the other men, all seated crosslegged like

Indians. They'd have a tough time getting up once the fireworks started, especially in the dark. He had one guy to worry about, and that guy was Bugs, and that guy was big, and that guy didn't get the name Bugs for nothing. There was a "Bugs" in Harlem, too, and the kid was as loony as April Fool's Day.

"Come on, punk," Bugs said. "Take the coffee."

"I don't want it," Johnny said.

"You see?" one of the men said. "You hurt his feelings."

"Aw, you take the coffee," Bugs said. "Here, punk, take the coffee. You drink it and get nice and warm, and then we'll see about paying for it. Go ahead, kid."

"Go ahead, kid," Harry said eagerly, thankful for the substitute Johnny had presented. "Go ahead, kid, drink it."

Johnny wet his lips and moved closer to the glowing grill. Bugs eyed him steadily, a stupid, vacuous smile on his face.

"All right," Johnny said nervously. "Give me the cup and I will."

Bugs extended the steaming tin cup. "That's a good little punk," he said. "That's the way we like it. No arguments. Now go ahead and drink your coffee, punk. Drink it all down fine. Go ahead, punk."

He handed the cup to Johnny, and Johnny felt the hot liquid through the tin of the container, and then he moved.

He threw the coffee into Bugs's face, lashing out with his left hand. He heard Bugs scream as the hot liquid scalded him, and then Johnny's foot lashed out for the grill, kicking wildly at it, hooking the metal under the glowing coils. The grill leaped into the air like a flashing comet, hung suspended at the end of its wire, and then the wire pulled free of the outlet, and the grill plunged down, and another man screamed. The grill glowed hot for an instant, with the man still screaming so that Johnny knew he'd been burned, too, and then the orange glow began to dwindle and the coils turned pale.

152

He did not hang around for the Technicolor exhibit. He started to run.

He passed Bugs, and Bugs screamed and grabbed for his right arm. He felt the big man's fingers close just below the elbow, and he opened his mouth, but his own scream was drowned in the bedlam around him. He threw his fist at Bugs's face, but the man clung to his arm, and he felt the tightening fingers there, felt the cut rip open in protest. He began to get weak. He felt his head spinning, and he kept throwing his left fist at Bugs's face, but Bugs would not let go. The arm felt as if it would fall off now. He knew he had to do something. The other men were getting to their feet now.

He kicked out. He brought his knee up into Bugs's groin, and Bugs let out a yell, and then the fingers magically dropped from Johnny's arm. He staggered across the room, wondering if he'd make it. He heard Bugs yelling wildly behind him, and he heard footsteps, and he could hear the low moaning of the man who'd been burned by the kicked grill. He headed for the steps, his arm throbbing and aching, with the sounds angry behind him, the footsteps thudding against the hard floor. His own feet hit the iron rungs of the steps, and he started down, hearing the clattering, resounding footsteps above him, clanking down the steps, like the distorted sounds in a terrible nightmare, down, down to the main floor and then across the darkened room with the piled dusty furniture and the shouts and cries behind him all the way. He leaped up for the window and worked it open, and then shoved the loose bar aside.

"I'll kill that black bastard!" he heard Bugs shout, but he was already outside and sprinting for the fence. He jumped up, forced to use both arms, and he saw the wild blood streak he left on the fence, and that was when he knew his arm had started bleeding again. He panicked for a moment, and then he was over the fence and dropping to the sidewalk, just as Bugs squeezed through the loose bar in the window.

He was tired, very tired. His arm hurt like hell now, and his heart exploded against his rib cage, and he knew he could not risk a prolonged chase with Bugs behind him, because the bastard would surely catch him.

He was at the corner now, and Bugs still hadn't reached the fence. He spotted the manhole, and he ran for it quickly, stooping down and expertly prying open the lid with his fingers. He'd been in manholes before. He'd been in them when the kids used to play stickball, and a ball rolled down the sewer and the only way to get it was by prying open the manhole cover and catching it before it got washed away to the river.

He was in the manhole now, and he slid the cover back in place, feeling it wedge firmly in the caked dirt, soundlessly settling back into position. He clung to the iron brackets set into the wall of the sewer, and he could hear the rush of water far below him where the sewer elbowed into the pipes. There was noise above him, the noise of feet tramping on the iron lid of the manhole. He held his breath because there was no place to go from here, no place at all.

The footsteps clattered overhead, and the iron lid rattled, and then the footsteps were gone. He waited until he heard more footsteps, figuring them to belong to the other vags who'd been with Bugs. And finally there was no sound overhead any more.

He was safe. They didn't realize he'd ducked into the manhole. They were probably scouting Third Avenue for him now, and they'd give up when they figured they'd lost him.

To play it doubly sure, he edged his way deeper into the sewer, holding to the iron brackets with his good hand. The stench of garbage and filthy water and the bowel movements of a giant metropolis reached up to caress his nostrils. He was tempted to move up close to the lid again, but it was darker down below, and if someone did lift the lid, chances were he wouldn't be seen if he went deeper.

The walls around him were slimy and wet, and the stink was all around him, like a soggy, vile blanket that smothered him. He felt nauseous, and he didn't know whether the nausea came from the dripping slime of the sewer or his dripping arm, and he remembered then that his arm was bleeding again.

He clung to the brackets, and he watched the blood spread on the bandage, and he shook his head wearily and wondered what he'd done with the orange-crate stick he'd used for a tourniquet so long ago, so goddamned long ago.

But at least he was safe here, and Bugs and the boys were upstairs. Upstairs. The thought frightened him a little. He descended deeper in the manhole until the elbow of the sewer was just beneath his feet, and he could hear the rush of water loud beneath him.

He was very weary, more weary than he'd been in all his life. The weight of the entire city seemed to press down on him, as if all the concrete and steel were concentrated on this one hole in the asphalt, determined to crush it and him into the core of the earth.

He hooked his left arm onto one of the brackets, and he hung there like a Christ with one arm free. The free arm dangled at his right side, the bandage soaked through now, the blood running down and dropping into the rushing water below.

Drop by drop it hit the slimy surface of the brown water while Johnny hung from the rusted iron bracket, praying that no one would lift the manhole cover, wondering how long it would be before he could go up again. Drop by drop the blood mingled with the brown water, flowed into the elbow where manhole joined sewer pipe, rushed toward the river.

And the rat clinging to the rotted orange crate lodged in the sewer pipe turned glittering bright eyes toward the manhole opening, and his nostrils twitched as he smelled blood. His teeth gnashed together an instant before he plunged into the water and swam toward the source of the blood.

Chapter Fourteen

She tried to see beneath the skin of Harlem.

She tried to take her mind off the neons that tinted the night sky. She went up Beale Street, 133rd between Seventh and Lenox, the street that had been called Jungle Alley in the 1920's, the roaring show place that was supposed to contain the heart of Harlem, a phony gaudy street set up for those who had the loot. The old spots were gone now, all of them— the Nest, Mexico's, Pod's, and Jerry's. She stopped in at Dickie Wells's place, but Johnny wasn't there.

And then she hit all the bars, the big bars and the little ones, the ones with small combos and the ones with jukeboxes, and the ones with strippers and the ones without. She ignored the clink of glasses and the sounds of music. She studied the faces, and she knew there were about a milion Negroes in Harlem, more or less, and she knew that Johnny was one of them, and so she studied the faces. And because she studied the faces with such scrutiny, and because the opening of her coat occasionally revealed the long curve of her flank, she was mistaken for something else, and she got an offer in almost every bar she hit. She ignored the offers when she could. In one bar on Seventh, a man pulled her down onto his lap and thrust his hand under her coat, surprised when he found a silken robe and an almost non-existent bra, more surprised when he felt the sting of her hand on his face.

The music gave her a background. The music was the music of a dock hand singing to the moon on a New Orleans wharf. The music was the lonesome wail of a cotton-picker, the plaintive cry of a fugitive slave. The music was the blues, and the music was low and soft, or high and hot, the jazz that started with a black man's horn, the bop that flowed from ten tan fingers. She ignored the music. She was looking *under* the music, and under the sights and the sounds and the smells, the way someone will look under a rug for a missing coin.

And when she'd covered all the bars she knew, and all the bars she didn't know, she began hitting the diners and the all-night luncheonettes, and a few of the drugstores that were open. And she listened to the talk, but the talk did not penetrate because she was looking and not listening.

"This cat, he the end, man. He gi' me the skin, an' then he say, 'Boy, lay a deuce on me, I hungry.' I tell him to cut out, 'fore I slit him ear to ear, an' man, he disappear."

She looked, and she did not listen.

"What kind of a girl do you take me for, Jase?"

"Just a nice girl, that's all. A nice girl I'd like to take home to Mother. Right this minute."

"You ain't got no mother, Jase, and you know it."

She smelled the coffee, and she saw her reflection in the polished urns, and she saw the deep brown liquid spilling from the spouts.

"This number's a sure thing, Joe, I know it."

"There ain't no number's a sure thing."

"This one is, boy. It's on my Social Security card, an' it's on my girl's apartment door. Now if that ain't a sure thing, you tell me what is."

"Ain't nothin' sure but death and taxes."

She was cold. She should have put more on. But she walked, and she opened doors, and she looked, and she closed doors, and she walked again, because somewhere in Harlem there was Johnny.

"You missed the whole point what he was talkin' about."

"I heard him just the same as you did."

"He wasn't sayin' we should become communists. You hear him once mention communism?"

"No, he was too smart for that."

"He was only sayin' we shouldn't spit on Russia. That's what he was sayin'. He was sayin' Russia was our salvation, that's all."

"And that ain't communism, huh? Man, you don't know yo' ass from yo' elbow when it comes to politics."

"I listened to as many of these guys as you did."

"But you always miss the point. I can spot a communist at sixty paces. I can smell the bastards. Even their soapboxes are stamped, 'Made in USSR.'"

"You never saw that, man. Who you kiddin'?"

The talk, the endless talk, the small talk that occupied the long nights, and she did not hear the talk except as a background.

"Wun't nobody could fight like Louis, nobody."

"What about Wolcott?"

"He's a bum. Louis eat him up if he was in his prime."

"Yeah, well, Wolcott ate *him* up."

"That's 'cause he wun't in his prime. Man, when Louis was in his prime, wun't nobody could touch him. Nobody."

And then there was no more talk, because there were no more places to hit. There were only the streets then, and she took to the streets. The lights in the tenements were out. The street lamps threw their glare onto the asphalt. She could hear the click of her sequined slippers on the pavement, and once a horn blared at her as she crossed the street aimlessly, and someone shouted, "Hey, you damn fool, watch where you're going!"

She *was* watching. She was watching very carefully. She was watching the way people walked, the slope of their shoulders, the tilt of their heads, the clothing they wore. She was watching all these because she knew Johnny the way she knew herself, and she knew she could spot him by his gait, or the way he held his head.

She saw the empty faces, the hollow faces, the ones hopped to the ears. She saw these, and she recognized them instantly, the wide staring eyes, the slack lip, the faint smile, the expression of bewildered wonder. She searched the faces, and in those faces she saw the momentary release from living, the high that would keep its owner away above Harlem until the edge wore thin, and then there was always another needle, or another lump of white piled high on a mirror, waiting to be sniffed up into the head, waiting to blow off the top of a skull. And she saw the other men, The Men, in capital letters, The Men who served the hunger. She recognized them because The Man was always recognizable. The Man was someone you got to know in Harlem, because The Man held the key to the magic kingdom of dreams.

And there were those lying in the gutter or huddled in the doorways, and these were not hopheads. These had their own poison, and they took that through the gullet, and it burned out their stomachs and their intestines and it finally hit their brains until they began to corrode like rusted water pipes. She saw these, and she stopped at each one she saw, looking down into his face, hoping it was Johnny, and yet praying it would not be Johnny lying in the gutter. She walked, and she looked, and the streets were very dark now, and she was a little frightened. She heard a sudden footstep behind her, felt a hand on her arm, heard a whispered, "How much, baby?" She threw the hand off her arm, and she hurried away into the darkness, wondering, Do I look like a whore?

Only a whore walks the street at this hour. Only a whore or a woman looking for her man. But where do you look? Where else is there?

She knew he was not religious, but she tried the churches anyway, all of them, thankful for the open doors, hoping Johnny had wandered into one of those open doors. She tried Kings Chapel Pentecostal Assembly on Fifth Avenue, and she tried St. Philip's on West 134th, and the Metropolitan Baptist on 128th, and the Abyssinian Baptist on 138th, hitting the churches as she thought of them, doubling back over her own footsteps occasionally. She hit all the churches she could think of, and then she started with the storefront churches, but he was nowhere to be seen.

She went to the Harlem Branch of the Y on 135th Street, but he wasn't registered there. She tried the Lafayette Theatre, and she hung around outside the movie houses that were still open with the late shows, watching the people as they spilled onto the pavements. She hung around Harlem Hospital, and on a chance she went inside and asked if they had a patient named Johnny Lane, but they had no one by that name.

She didn't know where to go any more. She tried Mount Morris Park, frightened when she heard footsteps behind her. She ran all the way out of the park, but in spite of her fear, she tried the other parks, Morningside Park, and then St. Nicholas Park, but she didn't find Johnny.

The streets were deserted now, and the lonely click of her high heels frightened her. She did not want to give up, but she simply didn't know where else to go. Could he have left Harlem? Gone down into Wop Harlem, maybe, or Spanish Harlem? Had he left the city entirely? Or was he lying in some hallway with his arm bleeding? Where was he? Where?

She headed for the Kingdom of Father Divine on 126th Street. An angel named Heavenly Peace told her that she had not seen anyone answering to Johnny's description. She left the place, looking crosstown to where the warehouses were cluttered near Wop Harlem. She glanced at the high outline of the Triboro, and she thought about the Father Divine chant, "He has the world in a jug and the stopper in his hand," and she wondered where in that jug Johnny could be.

She headed east, mostly because she didn't know where else to go. She walked down 126th Street, her heels clicking on the pavement. She stuck to the middle of the street because the sidewalks were darker.

She did not expect to find him any more.

This is my life, he thought.

This sewer is my life. The stink and the stench of it, and the city pressing down on me, this is my life. And the bleeding arm, that's all part of it, because I've really been bleeding all of my life.

You get used to the stench after a while. After a while, the stench becomes just a part of living. When you know only the stench, then that's normality. You perfume it a little, but it can never hide the stink, and so you adjust to it, and it becomes a part of your life, and you begin to think the stink isn't so bad any more, you begin to think everyone lives with the slime in his nostrils.

There's only a small part of you that tells you the truth, but nobody listens to the truth. That small part tells you that the stink is something unnatural, and sometimes you hear that whispering part of you, and maybe you listen, but you try to squelch it because the only way to live with the terrible smell is to accept it.

The smell is a very real thing.

It's in your nostrils when you awake in the morning. And if you flush out your nostrils with water from the tap, the smell goes away only momentarily, and then it returns again, too soon, and you can't go blowing your nose all day. The smell stays with you. It's part of living. It's like living in a sewer, and that's why the sewer is not strange. Once you get used to the smell, the sewer is just like any other part of your life.

And the city up above, the weight of the city, that's not unusual, because the weight is always there. You can feel the city pressing down on you. You can feel it in the slab fronts of the tenements, crusted with the soot and gasoline fumes of a century, you can feel it in the rusted iron of a fire escape when you sit out there on a summer day and try to see the sky beyond the sloping fronts of the buildings. You can feel the heavy weight of the city everywhere, pressing on the walls of Harlem until you want to scream and get the hell out, anywhere, anywhere where you can breathe without the smell in your nose and the weight on your back.

You learn to carry the weight.

It's heavy at first, but you learn to carry it, and you learn the sound of a slammed door. You learn that sound well, because there are a lot of doors slamming, not so many doors as there used to be, but still a lot of doors, and they close on you, and that's when the weight becomes really unbearable, and that's when you have to try the hardest, just to stay alive.

You can hit the dream pipe if you like, but the dream pipe doesn't help much, only for a little while, and when the dream wears off, you're back in Harlem again. Dreams are very thin. Dreams can be bought for the price of a stick of tea, but you can't live in a dream, not if you really want to live. The dream is only another slow way of dying.

You can hit the gas pipe if the weight gets to be too much for you. You can substitute the stink of gas for the other stink, and maybe someone lighting a match will take half the tenement with you, but what do you care as long as the stink is dissolved with the explosion, as long as the weight is lifted from your back? You can get so tired of living, so very damn tired.

And yet you can't let go of it, because you're a man. Under all the pressing, heavy weight, under all the filth and the stench and the stink, there's a man. That was the funny part of it. You realized you were a man only after you were denied everything else. And being denied all else, you became a man, and *only* a man, and being only a man, you somehow ceased to be a man. It was illogical and paradoxical, but it was true. When you stripped a man down to only his manhood, you stole his manhood. You crushed it flat into the pavement.

He was crushed flat into the pavement now, but he had found a hole in which to hide. And if he could hang to the rung with one arm, if he could just hang

162

there until things got a little better, if they ever got a little better, if the bleeding stopped, if the people stopped chasing him, if he could come out and be Johnny Lane and not a cipher in a long list of ciphers, not a faceless, manless man in a community of other faceless, manless men, it would be all right. He would not get carried away to the river. He would not float among the garbage and the gasoline slick. If only he could hang on, even though he was bleeding, someday, sometime, maybe far off in the future, maybe his manhood would come back. Maybe he could be a man among other men, and by so being maybe he could be a real man again, and not a man forced to be *only* a man, naked in the streets.

Maybe. Maybe someday.

He listened to the rush of the water beneath his feet, and he listened to the hush of the city over his head, the occasional automobile passing. The city would be sleeping now, and the manless men in Harlem would be sleeping too, resting, relieved from the weight of the city for just a little while. He could not see the color of the water in the darkness. He could only hear its rush, and the rush sounded clean and sweet and cool, even though he knew it was dirty.

When he heard the other sound, he thought it was part of the water.

He clung to the rung in the sewer wall, and he listened, and the sound separated itself from the water, and for a moment he thought someone was trying to lift the lid of the sewer, until he realized the sound was coming from below him. He thought then that his foot had scraped against one of the rungs, but the sound persisted, and he listened to it and tried to make it out, tried to give it an identity as a sound.

It started as a scraping, but a scraping could mean anything. A million things scraped, but he was in a sewer, and so he tried to think of what could possibly make a scraping sound in a sewer. A hunk of wood lodged in the pipe, maybe, something like that. Ex-

163

cept that this scraping sounded like a scratching, like someone clawing at something, like ...

He heard a tiny squeak.

He looked down, but he saw nothing. He heard only the scratching, and then the squeak, not the squeak of metal or wood, but a curiously animate squeak, a squeak like ...

He saw the pin points of light then. Two glowing pin points of light. Two round marbles with glistening dots in them, sparkling dots of light, darting. He caught his breath. He knew he was looking into the eyes of a rat.

He was scared. The fear shot into his skull, seemed to crackle there like a loosed lightning bolt. He was goddamned scared. He remembered that time with the jar, with the mouse clinging to his finger. He remembered the terror he'd felt then, and thinking of the terror, and thinking of what was down there below him, he began to tremble.

He screamed aloud when the rat leaped onto his foot. He screamed and the echo of the scream bounced off the slimy walls of the sewer, fled down to the elbow, rushed away with the water, and then reverberated in the sewer pipe on its long way to the river, howling like a banshee, filling his eardrums.

He could feel the rat clinging to his shoe. He shook his foot, climbing up closer to the manhole lid, but the rat clung, and it seemed as if every nerve ending in his body had suddenly moved into his foot. He forgot the pain in his arm, and he forgot the rusted rough edges of the brackets as he climbed closer to the lid.

He heard the breath rushing out of his mouth, and he could feel his heart pounding wildly, reaching up into his skull until he thought his head would shake to pieces.

"Go away!" he screamed, but the rat clung and he shook his foot desperately, trying to climb at the same time, almost losing his grip. "Go away, go away!" he shouted, until the sewer threw back the shouts, multiplied them a thousand times, gave up a hundred thousand voices screaming, "Go away, go away!"

164

He looked down, seeing only those glittering, pin-pointed eyes below him, not able to see the rat's body in the darkness, only those eyes.

And then the rat began climbing up the tweed of his trousers, and the scream bubbled out of his mouth, real fear this time, terror that shook him. He kept screaming, screaming, until he couldn't scream any more, and then his head banged against the manhole cover, and he pushed up against it frantically, wedging his shoulders against the flat iron surface, trying to move it. He could not budge the cover. He tried it again, and he felt the rat's claws digging into his trousers, scraping against his flesh. He could hear the rat's thin breathing now, and he knew the rat had smelled the blood and was working up toward his arm.

"No," he said. "No, please. No, no. Please, no. No!"

He scrabbled against the manhole lid, throwing all his weight against it, unable to move it. The rat moved again, and he tried to scream, but no sound came from his mouth. He pushed upward with his shoulders again, and this time the lid moved a little, and a fine sifting of dirt trickled down onto the back of his neck.

He shoved again, and then tried to brush the rat off his leg. The rat clung, snapping at his hand, drawing fresh blood. He pulled back his hand to suck the wound, and then remembered that the rat's mouth had touched his hand, and yanked it away quickly. He could not breathe. The stink crowded into his throat, and his lungs seemed full, too full; they couldn't possibly hold any more air. He was babbling now. He was saying, "No," and "Please," and "God," and "Go away," all in a meaningless jumble, not knowing what he was saying, knowing only that a rat was on his pants leg, knowing only that a rat had bitten his hand, knowing only that he could not move the manhole cover. He shoved at it again, desperately now, feeling it yield only slightly. His eyes widened. His jaw muscles tightened, and he felt the cords in his neck stand out.

He shoved at the cover again, putting all of his

strength into it this time, clinging to the bracket with one hand, and shoving his shoulders and his back and his head against the stubborn iron lid.

It moved aside. He almost didn't realize it. It moved aside, and the light from the street lamps splashed down into the manhole, illuminating his trouser leg and the rat.

It was a big animal, nine inches or so, not counting the tail. It was covered with matted, filthy fur, and the sight of the rat sent his spine up into his cranium. But the manhole lid was off now, and he thrust his head above the surface of the street, not caring about Bugs or his friends, not caring about anything now, only wanting to get away from the rat.

The rat pounced onto his arm, its teeth sinking into the sodden bandage. Johnny flipped up onto the asphalt, and the rat clung, only now Johnny didn't have to worry about holding onto an iron bracket. He balled his left fist, terror shrieking inside him, and he brought it down on the rat's head. He hit the rat again, and again, and again, feeling the squirming body under his fist, but the teeth seemed sharper now, clinging, biting, tearing flesh.

He got to his feet and ran across the street, stopping alongside the brick wall of a building. And then he began battering the bleeding arm against the brick, over and over again, slamming the tenacious rat against the wall, feeling each successive blow rumble up his arm, explode inside his head.

And at last the rat's jaws loosened and it fell away to the pavement, a whimpering ball of fur with a long, twitching tail. He did not look down at the rat. He was crying now, crying as he'd never cried in his life. The sobs started deep down within him, and they racked his body as he ran.

He ran west, wanting to get back to Harlem, wanting to get away from the broken body of the rat. He kept running, not seeing anything, the tears in his eyes blinding him. He ran, and he kept sobbing, and he kept

wondering why he'd had to run all his life, all his goddamn life.

And then he stopped running and fell to the pavement, unconscious.

Chapter Fifteen

She found him at three-ten in the morning, and she brought him home to Molly. The apartment was very cold, and Molly kept a quilted robe on, and Cindy did not remove her coat. The linoleum on the floor was dirty, but not because Molly had not scrubbed it. It was dirty because the filth had imbedded itself deep in the linoleum's pores, and no amount of scrubbing would ever get it out. The kitchen was black with the grease and soot of countless cookings. The windows were clean, but the paint on the window sills and sashes was chipped and cracking with old age.

The smell of urine from the hallways permeated the walls of the apartment. The cooking smells were there, too, and the smell of the gas stove, which had a very small leak. There was a calendar on the kitchen wall, and the calendar showed a picture of four monkeys playing poker. There was no other picture on the walls.

There were chairs and a table, but the wood of the table was scarred, and the chairs had broken rungs and backs. A radio set rested near the sink. The washtub was alongside the sink, and the washtub was used for baths whenever a bath was needed, whenever there was hot water.

They took Johnny into the other room, the bedroom, and then they called the doctor. The doctor came in ten minutes, a tall Negro who lived on the Golden Edge. He sniffed at the apartment, and then went in to see Johnny.

Molly and Cindy waited in the kitchen.

He was with Johnny for fifteen minutes. When he came out, he closed the bedroom door behind him and sat down at the table to write out a prescription.

"How is he?" Cindy asked.

"The arm is bad," the doctor said. "I gave him a shot of penicillin, but I'm not sure that'll do the trick."

"What do you mean?"

"Well, we may have to amputate."

"Amputate? What's he going to do without his right arm? How can he possibly do anything without his arm? You don't really mean . . ."

"We'll have to watch and see. It's a little early to tell now." The doctor paused. "His hand is bitten, too. The same kind of bite that's all along his arm. Maybe a dog . . ." He shook his head.

"But will he be all right?"

"Will he live, do you mean? Yes, he'll live. He's lost a lot of blood, and he's suffering from shock and exposure, but he'll live. He may be a little delirious during the night. He was mumbling something about bugs and rats and boats. I imagine he had a rough time."

Cindy nodded and bit her lip.

"I've given him something to make him sleep, and I want you to fill this prescription in the morning, and give him two capsules if he has any trouble sleeping any time tomorrow. I'll drop around again sometime in the afternoon to see how he's doing."

"All right," Cindy said dully.

"The important thing now is rest."

"The arm . . ."

"If it has to be amputated, we'll take him to a hospital. You don't have to . . . Well, what I mean to say, there are a lot of men who are useful citizens of our community, men without arms or legs, men with even more severe handicaps. It isn't the worst—"

"Black men?" Molly said softly.

The doctor eyed her levelly. "Black men," he said. He put the cap back on his fountain pen and rose.

"How much is that, Doctor?" Cindy asked.

"You can pay me at the end of treatment," the doctor said. "I suggest you all get some sleep now. If the arm *is* infected . . . Well, we'll see."

He put on his overcoat, whispered, "Good night," and then left the apartment.

He awoke at five-twenty. He sat upright in his bed, and he clenched his fists and screamed, bringing Cindy and Molly to his bedside. He stared at them blankly, and then he sank back against the pillows and said, "Why do I have to keep running? Why? Why? Why?"

And because Cindy thought he was referring to Luis' death, she stroked his forehead and said, "The police found the killer, Johnny. It's all right now. It's all right."

And only Johnny Lane knew that it wasn't all right, and that maybe it would never be.